Ellie Foster's
English Coursework

Tina Orr Munro

Ellie Foster's
English Coursework

Tina Orr Munro

RICKSHAW
PUBLISHING

A Rickshaw paperback

First published in Great Britain in 2011 by Rickshaw Publishing
Ltd, 102 Fulham Palace Road, London W6 9PL

www.rickshawpublishing.co.uk

A CIP catalogue record for this book is available from the
British Library.

ISBN 978-0-9565368-1-5

Cover designed by Anthony Grech-Cumbo

Printed and bound in Great Britain for Rickshaw Publishing Ltd
by CPI Group (UK) Ltd, Croydon, CR0 4YY

RICKSHAW
PUBLISHING

Acknowledgements

I'd like to say a very big thank you to Jo and Paul and everyone at Rickshaw Publishing for turning my dreams into reality. My thanks also to Sam, my editor, for his gentle advice and suggestions which hadn't occurred to me, but all made perfect sense. I'd like to thank my husband, Richard, for his unwavering support and his absolute belief in me when I had none, but most of all for making me laugh. And finally, thank you to Frank, Rosie, Joseph and Alice for being you.

For Rosie, Marie...and Mick

PREFACE

(Not sure what a preface is exactly, but I think it's a posh word for introduction.)

I've never really understood the point of keeping a diary. I spend much of my time trying to forget the many calamitous events that make up my life – why on earth would I want to write them down to be remembered forever? *(Calamitous – what a great word, by the way! I found it in my Oxford School Thesaurus, which was propping open my bedroom door. The book, though fabulously dull, could be useful if I'm to impress the examiner so I've decided to keep it handy. Duller and less useful Biology GCSE textbook now holding said door in place. I'll explain all about the examiner later.)*

Then Miss Bartlett, my English teacher, pointed out that I had managed to reach the end of Year 10 without completing any coursework for my English GCSE, which even she admitted was an achievement in itself, but not one likely to help me pass my exams.

I like Miss Bartlett. She's an NQT, that's Newly Qualified Teacher, which means she has only been teaching for a short while and still wants to be popular with the kids so she never shouts at us or gives us detentions or anything. She also lets us watch DVDs at the end of term. Well, she did until Nancy McDermott brought in American Pie. We'd watched almost half of it when Miss B realised it wasn't about cooking at all and turned it off.

Anyway, nice Miss Bartlett suggested that it would be good to do some coursework. I replied that, as it was the last day of the summer term, I really didn't have time to think about it and I would turn my attention to the matter just as soon as I got back to school in September. But she politely reminded me that if I didn't do any I would fail my English GCSE, which struck me as a bit over the top. By now, I must admit I was getting a bit bored of the conversation so I was quite pleased when she changed the subject.

Miss Bartlett: Are you going on holiday this summer, Ellie?

Great, I thought, she's dropped the coursework thing.

Me: Yes Miss, I am going to Greece with my mum and er...some others. *(No need to bore her with the details.)*

Miss Bartlett: That sounds lovely, why don't you keep a diary while you're away?

Me: What for, Miss?

Miss Bartlett: You could use it as part of your English GCSE coursework.

Me: Oh.

I couldn't believe it. How sneaky of her! Surely they don't teach that sort of thing at teacher training college? And I thought Miss Bartlett was different from the rest of them, but she's not, she's just the same, maybe even more devious. I have a good mind to report her to the Education Minister or someone and have her put on charges of obtaining coursework through deception. *(Maybe I should take out that bit about Miss Bartlett. Teachers can be so touchy. Come to think of it, if I'm really going to write this as a diary there's likely to be lots I'm going to have to take out before I send it in.)*

On the bus on the way home, I related the whole sorry episode to my best friend Poppy.

Me: She only wants me to write a diary! Who does she think I am, Adrian Bloody Mole?

Poppy: Is he that boy in year 11? The one with the limp? Oh, look over there, what do you think? Definitely a five?

Me: What?

Poppy: Okay, perhaps that's a bit harsh. A six then.

Me: What are you talking about?

Poppy: That cute guy down there, walking his dog. I give him six out of ten; he's going a bit thin on top, but he's got a nice bum. Sorry, what were you saying?

Me: Diary. Miss Bartlett says I should write a diary about my holiday for my coursework.

Poppy: Nosey cow. She just wants to find out about your life so she can use it against you.

Me: I know. It's bad enough that I'm forced to go on holiday with HIM and his awful kids, now I have to write about it.

Poppy: Don't look now, but Johnnie Watts has just got on the bus. Omigod, isn't he lush?

Me: I don't know, you told me not to look. So what do you think I should do?

Something told me Poppy wasn't giving my dreadful predicament *(another great word, never knew a thesaurus could be so useful)* her full attention and anyway, she was getting on my nerves.

Poppy: About what?

Me: My coursework, of course.

Poppy: Oh *that*! Download it off the Internet, like I do. (*Note to examiner: Poppy was joking, of course, and I can vouch for the fact that it is almost all her own work.*) Mmm, definitely a ten out of ten for Johnnie, don't you think? Catch ya later, Elles.

Poppy got up, tucked her skirt under her waistband until it barely hid her knickers and swayed down the bus aisle like Kate Moss on a catwalk to where Johnnie Watts was sitting. She slid coolly into the seat next to him, leaving me all on my own.

I let out a long sigh. How I wish I could be more like Poppy. She always looks fantastic. When she puts make up on, she glows. When I do it, I look like a circus reject. She takes everything in her stride. Boys, her Dad's wives, you name it, nothing fazes her. She is just so, so mature. Why can't I be more like that? If a boy so much as looks at me, I go bright crimson and start speaking Klingon. And as for my Mum's boyfriend, Trevor, well, where do I start?

With Poppy gone, I decided to draw up a list of the pros and cons of writing a diary about my holiday:

Pros:

- I will have completed some coursework, well for English anyway, which could turn my predicted, 'woeful' D grade (*my mother's words*) into a 'glorious' C grade (*my words*).
- It will give me a cast-iron excuse not to have to talk to the totally tedious Trevor (*is that alliteration? I'll have to check with Miss B, if she hasn't been sacked*) and the evil twins whilst on holiday.
- The alternative is far worse. I will have to do the coursework when I get back to school:

  a) in my lunch hour and

b) on Shakespeare, in the form of a 2000-word essay on "Consider the extent to which Lady Macbeth's ruthless ambition dictates her husband's actions." (*Is this a crap question I see before me?*)

- Mum might buy me a new laptop or even an iPad to take with us, so that I can write it easily as we go along.

Cons:

- My holiday will be so dull, there'll be nothing to write about and I will spend the whole time stressing about my coursework and will still not have done any by the time I get back to school.
- It will leave me no time to meet Greek boys who Poppy says are lush, although this view is based on Ali who is gorgeous and works at Abra-Kebab-Ra on the High Road – and who I think is actually Turkish, not Greek.
- It is against my principles to undertake schoolwork during the official holiday period.
- Will have to write it the old-fashioned way, as never in a million years is Mum going to buy me a new laptop or an iPad.

I was mulling my list over when Poppy returned to sit next to me. The Pros had it, by a shade.

Poppy: So what d'you think?

Me: I don't think I've any choice but to keep a diary for the next two weeks. After all, if it's really bad I can just make it up as I go along. No one will know any different.

Poppy: No, silly, what do you think of Johnnie? He's only just gone and given me his phone number.

Me: Great. Does he have a brother?

Poppy: Actually, he does, he's called Michael. He's only eleven, but he's big for his age. He could pass for thirteen-ish.

Me: Thanks.

Poppy: Don't worry Ellie, you'll find someone. You're about to spend a fortnight in Greece. Greek boys love the English. They'll be falling over themselves for you. If you can't get a guy there, you can't get a guy anywhere.

Rub it in, why don't you?

Poppy: Besides, remember what we agreed?

Of course I remembered. I was hoping that Poppy had forgotten, but clearly she hadn't. Some weeks back during Food Technology we made a pact that we would both 'do it' while we were on holiday this summer. Poppy said it was the perfect opportunity to get the whole business out of the way, for two reasons:

a) Everyone else in my class has done it except Lucy Telling, who looks twelve and has yellow teeth and

b) as Poppy said: "If we do it on holiday, no one will be able to spread nasty rumours about us."

She had a point. Sandra Whitbread apparently did it with Jamie Harbinger at the Valentine's disco and everyone knew about it, even Miss Bartlett. Sandra denied it totally but no one believed her, poor thing. Jamie went round telling everyone he'd 'had better', which made it ten times worse, of course. It's one thing to do it but quite another to be told you are rubbish at it. Actually, I don't think Jamie Harbinger had had anything at all, but that didn't stop the gossip and Sandra ended up having loads of 'chats' with the school nurse, who has the bedside manner of Cruella de Vil. It was truly awful.

Poppy: This is my stop, Elles. Have a great holiday. Make sure you text me all the gory details. Remember, don't settle for anything less than an eight.

I watched Poppy get off the bus and wiggle her way towards a group of lads standing outside the Co-op. Why can't I do that? I walk miles out of my way to avoid groups of boys for fear that they may notice me.

I returned to my list. The gloom descended. Great! Not only do I have to spend two weeks in the company of my mother (just about bearable), my mother's boyfriend (frankly unbearable), his satanic children (plain scary) and their love child (highly strung), I also have to keep a diary about it all and find time to have sex with a boy who looks like Zac Efron.

Possible titles for my diary/English coursework:

- Misery *(I think that's been taken)*.
- My big, crap Greek holiday *(examiner may not like use of word 'crap')*.
- My family and other weirdos *(definitely in the running, although Greek people are probably perfectly sane, in which case it's rude)*.
- Me, my mum, her boyfriend, his kids, their love child *(too confusing)*.

Perhaps the title will come to me as I'm writing my diary. In the meantime, here it is: *Ellie Foster's English Thingy*. I still don't understand the point of a diary but hopefully it'll be worth a C, at least.

DAY ONE

4.00am – (Yes, that's AM.)

We've set off from Hollis Street in Norbury. Where's Norbury? Well, it's a cruddy little place in South London. My mum and I moved there when she split up from Dad and I've never forgiven her. The least she could have done to ease the pain of their divorce is move to somewhere cool like Islington, or Camden, or even Stoke Newington, at a push. But no, she chose Norbury. Not so much up-and-coming, as down-and-left-ages-ago. As far as I can tell, Norbury is famous only for deserted launderettes smelling of pee *(is urine a better word?)* and burnt-out bookies *(is that more alliteration? Good to get it in early, just in case examiner doesn't have time to read entire coursework)*. Oh, and we have a resident rapist *(more alliteration, I'm on a roll)* whose identity has kept the men and women *(important to appear PC – get it – PC?)* in blue guessing for the last five years, which has suited my mother no end.

Common conversations with my mother:

Mum: Ellie, where do you think you're going?

Me: Just popping to the shops.

Mum: No way, not on your own. Not with that sex maniac on the loose.

Me: Mum, it's 3.30 in the afternoon and you can call him a rapist, I do know what it means.

16

Mum: Give me a minute, I'm coming with you.

Me: I bet they don't have rapists in Islington.

So, thanks to Norbury's resident rapist, or rather my mother's belief that he lurks permanently by the Clearasil counter in Boots ready to pounce on me, I am under a constant curfew. On the odd occasion that I do manage to leave the house I'm trailed by my mother muttering on about how appalling it is that a fifteen-year-old (*nearly sixteen*) knows the meaning of the word rapist.

Anyway we set off from cruddy Norbury at stupid o'clock and are now heading to the airport to catch our flight to Greece.

I am sandwiched in the back of the car between the love child, who is strapped into the baby seat and Blue, one half of the evil twins (*he's a boy, in case you were wondering*). His sister, Skye (*I kid you not*), is sat on the other side of him, by the door. With their matching tangerine hair, manic grins and wild eyes, they look like Chucky's less stable brother and sister. (*Obviously, I haven't seen Child's Play 1, 2 or 3, or Bride of Chucky or Seed of Chucky as they're all rated 18. A friend – whose name I can't remember and who happens to be very good at describing things – once told me about them.*) In the front passenger seat is Mum, who is dressed in khaki combat trousers, a denim jacket and one of those red and white checked scarves the Arabs wear to stop sand getting into their eyes. I can't help but let out a heavy sigh and shake my head in disbelief. This is the same woman who once told me only cowboys looks good in denim and that khaki should be seen only on the battlefield! Clearly, this is just another example of the Svengali-like hold HE has over her (*I learnt about Svengalis in Art History. Apparently, Picasso was one – or was it Salvador Dali?*). Mum's best friends used to be Nicole Farhi and Jimmy Choo, until HE turned up. Now it's all tie-dye T-shirts and bandanas. Mum says she feels more comfortable in 'fair trade' gear, but there's nothing fair about your own mother wearing a kaftan and moccasins to

17

Parents' Night. That's just cruel.

HE, Trevor, my mum's boyfriend, is driving us. His long, receding hair is scraped back into a weedy ponytail and he is wearing a thick, cream CARDIGAN. And he has a goatee. Oh God, why me? Every now and then I catch my Mum and Trevor exchanging a smile. He even put his hand on her knee. How repulsive, behaving like a couple of Year 8's. What does my mother see in him? Maybe he's drugging her or something. I wonder if her rapidly deteriorating fashion sense is enough evidence to go to the police with.

The fact that it is four in the morning is reason enough to be miserable, but the situation has just got a whole lot worse. My mother has started singing. In an effort to be modern and 'with it' she is attempting to sing *Walking on Sunshine*, which is ancient and 'past it'.

Unfortunately, walking on sunshine is the only line of the song she knows. Every now and again she blurts it out at the top of her voice. Then there's a lull until she belts it out again. She sounds like she has got a non-swearing, optimistic strain of Tourette's syndrome (*like that guy that won* Big Brother *a few years ago – though his strain wasn't so non-swearing. Or optimistic*). Let's hope she tires of this by the time we reach the airport and she comes into contact with normal members of the public and the security services.

4.15am

We're stuck in a traffic jam, near the airport.

Thankfully, Mum has stopped shouting 'sunshine' every 30 seconds after she woke the love child who is now whimpering in fear. She is now muttering about telling SOMEONE we should have left home earlier.

Trevor: Elaine, our flight's not until 9.00am. We're only half a mile away. We'll be on time, even if we cartwheel the rest of the way!

Me: There's no need to be sarcastic. Mum's got a point. *(Trevor shoots me a look in the mirror.)*

Mum: It's okay, Ellie, Trevor's right. I'm panicking as usual.

Traitor! How has it come to this? My own mother is ganging up against me with this bangle-wearing hippy! Two years ago, it was just me and Mum. We were happy. We used to cuddle up together on the sofa and Mum would tell me 'you and me girl, against the world' and 'we don't need anyone else, we're fine and dandy just as we are' *(whatever dandy means)*. Every time she did a job she thought was man's work, like putting the bins out or filling the car with petrol, she would punch the air and shout 'girl power' *(which was all right at home but was excruciatingly embarrassing on the forecourt of the local Texaco garage)*.

Then one day Mum told me she had a boyfriend. It felt like someone had punched me in the face. I was stunned, speechless. What happened to 'all men are scum'? I tried to be cool about it, heavy scenes aren't my style. But inside I was screaming with indignation *(great word)* and hurt.

Me: Mum, you're almost 40 years old. You're too old for a boyfriend.

Mum: I'm 38, thank you very much. All right then, manfriend.

Me: Manfriend? That's even worse.

Obviously, I immediately sought Poppy's advice. She has bags of experience with parents dating. Her mum ran off when she was three and her dad changes his wives more often than his cars (*he owns a garage*). Poppy told me that Mum's 'manfriend' was taking advantage of the fact she was RD (*recently divorced*) and that he had most certainly conned her into going out with him by taking her out for expensive meals and showering her with lavish gifts. Poppy was right. I checked my Mum's drawers where I found a packet of lavender joss sticks and a menu for Keen Bean, the local veggie takeaway. I tried to warn Mum that her manfriend was trying to 'buy' her love but she accused me of overreacting. Then when she didn't mention him again, I assumed that she had come to her senses and chucked him. (*Will examiner be familiar with 'chucking' in the relationship sense? Perhaps 'ended the relationship' sounds better.*)

4.25am

Standing in the front of the queue for check-in. And there's not a soul in sight. Probably because it's still two hours before the desk opens. Mum has taken the love child to the baby-changing room. The evil twins are charging at each other with trolleys.

Trevor (*in what I'm sure he thinks is a very firm voice*)**:** Blue. Skye. Don't do that, you might hurt each other.

I thought that was the general idea. The evil twins abandon the trolleys instantly.

Trevor: You see, Ellie, it is possible to reason with young children. They respond more positively than if you scream and shout and threaten them.

Me: Right. Perhaps you should ask them nicely not to run the wrong way up the escalator.

Trevor: What? Oh for God's sake! Blue, Skye! Get over here now!

Me: They don't seem to be able to hear you. It's okay, the security guard's got them.

A huge man with square shoulders and a shaved head (*definitely no more than a three*) peels the two struggling eight-year-olds off the escalator handrail and marches them back towards us.

Security: Sir, do these two belong to you?

Trevor: Yes.

Security: Please control them. The airport is not a playground.

Trevor: Yes, officer.

Then he turns to Blue and Skye and says in a *sotto* voice (*I learnt that in music, hopefully a bit of Italian will impress examiner*):

Trevor: If you don't behave, you will have to sit on the naughty step for three minutes.

Three minutes? Is that all? When I get told off I get sent to my bedroom for days.

Skye: But the naughty step's at home.

Trevor: Well, I'll find another one.

Blue: Where? There's only escalators here. Can we sit on the escalator, please, please?

Trevor (*fortissimo*)**:** No, just belt up and behave.

☆ ☆ ☆ ☆ ☆

4.27am

Mum has just returned with the love child and told Trevor off for letting Blue and Skye 'run riot'. Brilliant; we haven't even checked in and they're at each other's throats.

Mum: I could hear them from the toilets, Trevor. It's not good enough. You must keep them under control.

Trevor: They were just letting off steam, Elaine, they weren't doing anyone any harm. Control is a very dangerous approach to child-rearing, if you don't mind me saying so, Elaine. Control is exactly what governments try and exercise over us every day of our lives. Control is what the Nazis did in Germany in the 1930s and look where it got them. Control is another word for oppression and that needs to be fought at all costs.

Oh God, why me? I half expect him to shout out 'You can take our lives, but you can never take our freedom', like Mel Gibson in *Braveheart*. Actually, the idea of Trevor being hung, drawn and quartered is quite appealing (*and Mel Gibson still gets a nine, despite being ancient*).

Mum: All I'm saying, Trevor, is that they may hurt themselves or get lost if we don't keep an eye on them.

Sounds good to me.

Trevor: Well, that's a different matter. And I see your point.

4.35am

The love child is asleep. Satan's spawn are sucking noisily on my boiled sweets. Trevor is sulking over a cup of Lapsang Souchong. He has now accused Mum of poisoning the twins by feeding them pear drops and pineapple chunks but as Mum quite rightly pointed out, if she hadn't they would both still be on the luggage carousel.

Trevor: But they're packed with additives. It just turns them hyper, Elaine.

Mum: To be honest, Trevor, I doubt anyone'll notice any difference.

Well said Mum. At this rate, we won't even reach the departure lounge. With any luck, we should be heading home by seven and Trevor and his odious children will be history.

Oh no, Trevor's looking at me. I feel an attempt to bond with his girlfriend's insolent (*good use of an adjective*) fifteen-year-old (*nearly sixteen*) daughter coming on.

4.40am

It gives me no pleasure to report I was right.

Trevor: What are you writing, Ellie?

Me: English project.

Trevor: Really? That's excellent. Very dedicated of you. You've got her well trained, Elaine. Wish my students were as committed as you.

Me: Right.

Trevor: Let's see if you know this one, Ellie. What sea separates Italy and Greece?

Me: Dunno. Atlantic?

Trevor: Good guess. No, it's the Adriatic.

Me: Right.

Perhaps I should reveal at this stage that Trevor is a Geography teacher which, according to him, is the most important subject on the National Curriculum. On our first meeting he asked me to name the mountain range that sits between Europe and Asia. We were at Pizza Express in Soho (*Norbury isn't posh enough for a Pizza Express*).

It was just after we had ordered a drink that my mother revealed she was in fact still seeing her 'manfriend' and that they had become 'close' and that it was time I should meet him too. I should have realised something was up when she said she had booked a table at Pizza Express. She took me there when she told me that she and Dad were splitting up. Sloppy Giuseppes have very negative associations for me.

Anyway, I met Trevor for the first time. He was wearing jeans and a black waistcoat (*seriously*) and looked like that guy out of that group where two old guys bounce up and down with guitars like they've got dementia – Status Quo? Anyway, he shook my hand and told Mum and I that we looked more like sisters than mother and daughter. Mum actually blushed; oh dear. Then he decided that the best way to win me over was by asking me Geography questions. I have always loathed Geography. It is pointless. Who cares if one third of the world's population is Chinese? Just strikes me as boasting. Anyway, I dropped the subject at the end of Year 9 but I couldn't be bothered to tell Trevor, who has kept on with these bonding exercises where he tests my knowledge and then tries to hide his horror at how little I know. The answer, by the way, is the Urals separate Europe and Asia (*I don't want the examiner to think I am thick or anything*).

7.25am – Departure lounge.

Our flight is delayed by three hours. The love child is bawling its head off. Know how it feels. Mum is muttering about having an extra few hours in bed if SOMEONE had checked the flight details on the internet before we left the house.

Trevor has tried to avert what must be an imminent bust-up between him and Mum by taking the savages to Holland & Barrett to stock up on pumpkin and sunflower seeds to 'try and counteract the damage done by the boiled sweets'.

Mum (*in a loud voice to drown out cries of love child*): So Ellie, having a good time?

Me: Great.

Mum: Don't be like that, it's no one's fault the flight is delayed. We'll be there soon enough. Okay love, shhh now.

Me: I'm not bothered about the flight. I would rather stay in Norbury anyway.

Mum: There there, love, it's okay, stop crying. Ellie, can you smile a bit more? I think your scowling is upsetting the baby.

Me: Gat getter?

Mum: That's it, shhh love, no more tears now. Look Ellie, this trip is important.

Me: Gaybe gor goo, gut got gor gee.

Mum: Pardon? Okay, you can stop smiling now. You've cheered up now, haven't you gorgeous? No, it's important for all of us. A real chance for us to be all together as a -

Me: Family?

Mum: A unit is what I was going to say.

I should point out that although Trevor and Mum have produced the love child between them, they don't live together; thanks to me. Mum tentatively suggested it just before the birth of said love child, but I threatened to go straight out and buy a kilo of scag (*maybe I should change that to heroin, in case examiner is unfamiliar with latest narcotic terminology*) and hang around various chemists until the resident rapist chanced upon me. Anyway, it did the trick and Mum decided Trevor should stay in his flat in Streatham 'for the time being' while Mum, the love child and me live in our scuddy place in scuddy Norbury.

7.45am

Wow, I have written loads.

Even with all the personal bits removed, there is reams left.

Perhaps I've written enough for my coursework although I have the feeling something is missing. A middle, perhaps. Oh, and an ending. Hopefully, the flight will be cancelled altogether and that problem will be solved.

7.50am

I have been left in charge of the sleeping love child.

Trevor has taken the evil twins to WHSmith. Mum has gone with them but she really wants to go to Duty-Free. I have caught her throwing furtive looks at the fags. (*Trevor thinks she gave up shortly after they met. He's more stupid than I thought.*)

I decided to text Poppy even though I promised myself I would wait until I reached Greece; I am so miserable and Poppy always cheers me up. She is in Sorrento with her dad and his fourth wife, who is 23. It's enough to send anyone into lifelong therapy but Poppy just laughs it off. She says every new wife is an opportunity to better her lifestyle. She calls them guilt gifts: while her dad is spending time trying to impress his latest girlfriend, Poppy gets anything she asks for. So far, she has seen Beyoncé twice, got a new pony and a whole new wardrobe from Zara. I decided to try the same tactic with my mother. I casually mentioned to her one day that I hardly ever saw her anymore because of the amount of time she was spending with Trevor. I felt a bit mean, as she was genuinely upset and concerned. I came home from school the next day to find two cinema tickets for the director's cut of *Gandhi* and a copy of *York Notes: Macbeth* lying on my bed.

TEXT TO POPPY:

Bored, bored, bored.

Having crap time!
What about you?

TEXT FROM POPPY:

Having great time.
Already snogged the
sous-chef, who's at
least 18. Plan to do it
tomorrow...

No! No! No! I can't believe it. She only left for Sorrento yesterday and she has already snogged someone. By Saturday, she will have done it and I'll be the only one in the class (*apart from Lucy Telling*) who hasn't even hit the ball, let alone got to first base.

Although Poppy doesn't know this, I haven't even done 'tongues' with a boy. If she knew what a sexual misfit I was, she would ditch me and find a cooler friend. (*I've just realised that at fifteen, Poppy may be about to break the law. Must remember to remove above paragraph in case examiner calls the cops or the SS...that's social services, not group belonging to 1930s fascist regime – good display of historical knowledge, could get me an extra mark or two, perhaps I should leave this in after all.*)

TEXT TO POPPY:

Well done!

(*Well, what else are you meant to say on these occasions?*)

Right, now, I am mega-miserable. Stuck in an airport with a screaming baby (*okay, love child is asleep at the moment, but that's out of character*), a couple of demonic eight-year-olds, a deluded mother who thinks it's 1963 and her moronic boyfriend who thinks yaks' wool is fashionable. On top of that, I am now under pressure to 'do it' with the first person I clap eyes on or lose my best friend in the whole world. Life stinks.

The 'unit' has just returned with a plastic WHSmith's bag.

Trevor: A cornucopia (*check spelling and meaning*) of goodies. I got *Reiki for Beginners* and *Raising Confident Children*. Your mum got *A Suitable Boy* by Vikram Seth. A terrific book.

I raise an eyebrow at Mum, who pretends to read the book sleeve.

Me: Didn't they have any Danielle Steel in stock?

Mum: I don't know, I didn't look. I've been meaning to read this for ages.

Trevor: Blue and Skye, I've got you Tolkein's *The Lord of the Rings* for early readers. And we got you a little something, too, Ellie.

Me: Really?

Trevor: A 1001 questions you have always wanted to ask.

Me: Is the first question, why are you such a prat? (*Okay, I didn't say that. In fact, I didn't come up with it until later, after the shock had worn off.*)

Mum: Well Ellie what do you say?

Me: Um, thanks.

Mum: Right Ellie Foster, you and I are going to have a little chat.

Mum grabs my arm and marches me off in the direction of Duty-Free. When we are out of earshot of the others, we stop and she hisses at me.

Mum: You can at least try to look as if you are enjoying this holiday. After all, you did choose to come with us.

Not strictly true, although as far as my mother is concerned it is (*let's hope she doesn't read this*). I had actually asked Dad if I could go with him and his muse (*good use of our Beloved Bard's own language, found the word in my trusty thesaurus which has also come along for the ride*) who is called Delphine. She sounds posh, doesn't she? As it happens, she did grow up on an estate, but it's in Catford. My Mum says she's as rough as houses (*is that a simile?*), although she did add that at least Delphine paid attention in Sex Ed classes and doesn't have four kids by four different dads who are 'ASBO'd up to their eyeballs for setting fire to their elderly neighbours'. I think that's called a back-handed compliment (*is that a literary term?*).

Actually, try as I might, I can't dislike Delph. She is laid back and fun with her bright plum hair – 'naturally-dyed, darling'. I think Dad likes her for all the reasons I do and possibly a couple more as she has humongous (*is that a real word, if not, do I get extra marks for introducing new words into the English language? Must check with Miss B*) breasts which she makes the most of by wearing T-shirts cut so low it's hard to concentrate on her face when she speaks. I find myself staring down her chest so often, I asked Poppy if she thought I might be becoming a lesbian. But Poppy said it was more likely I was 'bi' which is totally cool and 'in' at the moment and she then got really sulky because she hadn't thought of it first.

Anyway, I asked Dad if I could go with him and Delph to Spain. Dad said yes, but when he checked with the holiday company he had booked with, he found that it didn't allow kids. I tried to persuade him that I wasn't a kid anymore, but he promised to make it up to me and let me come on holiday with them next year. I didn't tell Mum any of this as I didn't want her to think that she was my second choice. I then felt a bit guilty because she looked really chuffed when I asked if I could go with her, Trevor and the rest of the zoo to Greece. She hugged me so hard she made me yelp, and then she started to sniff. It was all totally embarrassing.

Mum: Ellie, I am so pleased. You'll grow to love Trevor, Skye, Blue and our baby, just like me.

Famous last words. Stood outside the Duty-Free shop in the early hours (*8.00am is early hours in my book*), I can safely say my 'love' for Trevor and co hasn't even germinated (*learnt that in Biology; see, Mrs Duce, I do listen*), let alone started to grow.

Mum: Please Ellie, for my sake; try to get along with Trevor. He is really very fond of you.

How can she be saying this? What kind of voodoo has he used on her? I must remember to hide *Reiki for Beginners*. Clearly this is part of his master plan to keep Mum in his thrall. For now, I will just go along with her.

Me: Okay Mum.

Mum: Good, that's settled then. Now go back and thank Trevor properly for the book.

Me: What?

Mum: You heard me.

Me: But where are you going?

Mum nods towards Duty-Free.

Mum: I, er, have to nip in here to get some, er, perfume for your Gran.

Yeah, right. Say hi to your friend Nick O'Teen for me. She must think I was born yesterday. I return to where Trevor is sitting.

Me: Thanks, Trevor, for the book. It's...really nice.

He holds up a small paper bag.

Trevor: Pleasure. Pumpkin seed?

Me: No, thanks.

Trevor: Right Ellie, let's try this one for size, what is the IMF?

Me: Low-quality 90s pop band. Had a hit with *Unbelievable*.

Trevor: Good try, but no – I think that'd be EMF. IMF is the International Monetary Fund. You'll have to know that for your Geography GCSE.

Me: Right.

Before Trevor can ask me another pointless question an announcement over the tannoy calls passengers for flight 354 to Athens.

Trevor: Excellent, that's us. I'll help Blue and Skye with their belongings; can you take my man bag for me, Ellie?

Man bag! Poppy says that only gay men carry man bags. Perhaps I should tell Mum that her boyfriend prefers men. It would explain the ponytail.

12.05pm

The good news is we're finally on the plane. The bad news is I have been told to sit between Blue and Skye to stop them fighting. Mum, Trevor and the love child are sat behind us.

Me: If you don't talk to me for the whole trip, I'll let you have my jelly babies.

Skye: They make us hyper. I'm telling Trevor.

Me: Don't you mean Dad?

Skye: No.

Me: Look, these jelly babies are special, they're shaped like people and you can bite their heads off.

I demonstrate a decapitation of a purple jelly baby (*wow, decapitation, that's five syllables! Must be worth a B grade, at least*) and it seems to work. Skye grabs a handful of doomed sweets from the bag and I give the rest to Blue. Peace at last.

TEXT FROM POPPY:

Just had grope with
chef in linen cupboard!
Soooo sexy.

Blimey, she's rampant. I can't take this pressure. Still, can't be seen to let the side down.

TEXT TO POPPY:

Dishy air steward
giving me the eye.

TEXT FROM POPPY:

Not poss, air
stewards all gay.

Damn. I begin to text her back when the air steward in question approaches me. Perhaps he really does fancy me.

Air Steward: Excuse me mees. You must turn ze phone off. It interferes with ze navigation of ze plane.

Me: I'm only texting my friend.

Air Steward: I don't care if you're calling ze President of ze United States, you will turn it off now or get off ze aircraft.

Me: Okay, okay.

Really, some people (*adults, mostly*) get so stressy about nothing.

Mum: Really Ellie, I can't believe you just tried use your mobile phone on an aeroplane. How embarrassing. Everyone knows how dangerous that can be.

Embarrassing? She doesn't know the meaning of the word. Embarrassing is having your mother canoodling in your presence with a man who isn't your real father (*although if he was that would also be embarrassing*).

1.20pm – Frankfurt airport.

We are in Germany. We're meant to be going to Greece, but Trevor is such a cheapskate he booked us on Lufthansa, which goes to Athens via Frankfurt because it saved him £3.25. Because we were delayed at Heathrow, we have now missed our connecting flight to Athens. Great.

Trevor is queuing to get us on another flight while Mum has 'nipped to the loo' and I am lumbered with the rugrats who keep pushing the barriers and setting the alarms off and the love child who is sat on my lap emitting a strange smell.

Trevor, who is now at the front of the queue, has started talking very loudly to a very bored-looking stewardess.

Trevor: What do you mean the next flight isn't until 9.00pm? That's a disgrace.

The stewardess leans towards him to say something.

Trevor: No, I will not keep my voice down. I want everyone to know what appalling service I have received from your airline. I want a full refund to compensate for the terrible inconvenience you've caused us.

The stewardess murmurs something else.

Trevor: Food vouchers? Yes, well that's a start, I suppose. Thank you. Thank you very much (*which sounds slightly odd as he is still shouting*)!

I hope that Trevor's little 'scene' is over. Oh no – who's that lady? This is getting worse. Just as Trevor is pocketing his vouchers, a lady in a bright blue uniform and more makeup than a circus clown marches over to us and glares at me.

Lady: You move.

Me: Move? Where?

Lady: Somewhere else. This is departure gate for Ljubljana.

I look at the bags and the love child and suddenly feel helpless *(not only because I haven't a clue where or what Ljubljana is)*. Placing this level of responsibility on a fifteen-year-old can't be legal. At this point, Trevor returns.

Trevor: What's going on?

Me: This lady says we have to move.

Trevor turns to the woman with a face like granite.

Trevor: Really? And where do you suggest we sit? On the floor?

Lady: Yes.

Trevor turns beetroot.

Trevor: How dare you? You feed my children stale bread on the plane and then force us to sit on the floor. Well, thank you, Lufthansa, thank you very much indeed.

Lady: No problem.

Trevor: I was being sarcastic.

What a cheek the man has got! Pretending I am his daughter in a cynical ploy to get us all seats. Yes, I would prefer a chair to sitting on the floor, but that's not the point. Impersonating my natural father has to be illegal, doesn't it? (*Leave that bit in so examiner gets the hint and notifies the authorities).*

1.30pm

Mum has just returned from the toilet with a mouthful of Orbit, smelling very strongly of Chanel No. 5.

Mum: Why are you all sitting on the floor?

Me: Long story.

Trevor: It's alright, Elaine. I've told them the service is rubbish and Air France is much better. That cut deep; after all they're German.

Me: Isn't that stereotyping?

Mum scoops up the love child, who stops crying immediately and stomps up to the desk.

Mum: No child of mine sits on the floor. I demand you find us some seats.

Stewardess: Certainly madam. There is a restaurant downstairs, you can sit down there. Your husband already has been given ze vouchers. Er, can I remind you madam that smoking is strictly *verboten* anywhere in ze airport.

Mum then marches back to where we were all sitting cross legged on the floor.

Mum: Right, everyone follow me.

And we all traipse after her like Julie Andrews and the von Trapp family in *The Sound of Music* (*a film I loathe but am forced to watch every Christmas*).

Trevor: Elaine, are you still smoking?

Mum: Smoking? I am fuming, Trevor. How could you let them sit on the floor? (*Good deflection, Mum, but a relationship built on lies is doomed to fail.*)

We're now sat in the restaurant in silence. Well Mum, Trevor and me are silent. Love child is wailing and the evil twins are sticking chips up their noses. The air is thick with tension. Perhaps Mum is finally beginning to see Trevor for the total loser he is.

Trevor: Right Ellie, try this one: who discovered the Spice Islands?

Me: Schwartz?

Trevor: Not a bad attempt, but it was Magellan. I think she's getting better, Elaine.

Mum: I need the toilet. Look after the baby, will you?

DAY TWO (just)

1.00am – Athens airport.

We have made it. We are officially on Greek soil. Just. It may be the early hours of the morning but it is boiling hot. The place feels like an oven. Even Trevor has taken his cardigan off, to reveal a T-shirt with the words 'I am with this idiot...' and a picture of a finger pointing to left on it. Mum has dispatched him to find us some accommodation for the night. He did try to suggest that we spend the night in the airport and catch the first ferry in the morning, but he didn't get past 'Elaine, these seats look comfy enough why don't...'

The savages and the love child are all fast asleep, thank God. It's just me and Mum. I've forgotten what that feels like.

Mum: Nearly there, Ellie.

Me: Where?

Mum: Don't be like that. Your sullen attitude really isn't helping matters.

Me: No, seriously. I really don't know where we're going.

Mum: Perhaps if you showed a little more interest in what's happening around you, you would.

1.05am

Trevor has reappeared and told us he has found 'a nice little place'. Better not be a bus shelter.

Trevor: It looks perfect and right near the port, not to mention very reasonable.

Mum: Well done, Trevor, that's sounds great. Every cloud has a silver lining and all that. Right Ellie, you take the baby. I'll take Skye and you take Blue and we'll come back for the bags. Onwards and upwards. I knew you'd come through, Trevor.

Anyone would think Trevor has signed an agreement on world peace or something the way she carries on. He's only found a bloody hotel for the night by visiting a desk marked 'Hotel Accommodation'. Even he couldn't mess that up.

2.30am – We've finally reached the hotel.

Bloody hell. We've finally reached the hotel to discover Trevor has only booked one room; he is so mean. Plus it's baking hot. We've opened the windows, but it has made no difference. I'm so tired, I can't write anymore.

6.00am

Can't sleep. It's soooooooooo hot in here and I'm absolutely sweating gallons. I can't bear the heat, plus I am deeply uncomfortable at the thought of my mum and her moronic boyfriend sharing a bed in the same room as me. The fact that both the love child and Blue are wedged between them is not the point.

6.15am

Still awake. Still boiling hot. My head is pounding and my throat is parched. I am gasping. Just sat up and saw a glass of water by Mum's bed, like the holy grail in that Indiana Jones film. Felt a bit guilty as it was probably hers, but too thirsty to pass it up.

9.05am

So tired. I was woken up at 8.00am by Trevor standing above me, waving an empty glass. Good God, I thought, it's only a glass of water.

Trevor: Who drank my contact lens?

Oops.

Mum: What are you talking about?

Trevor: I couldn't find my contact lens stuff last night, so I put each lens into two separate glasses with a little bit of water, now one of them is empty.

Me: Omigod, I think I'm going to throw up.

Mum: Ellie, how could you? Of all the infantile things!

Me (*gagging*): I didn't do it on purpose. I was thirsty.

Trevor: It's alright Elaine. It's not Ellie's fault, I should've been more careful. I think we should all just calm down.

Brown-noser! (*Considering removing, don't want to shock the examiner.*) As if I need him to fight my battles for me! It's all very well for him to tell people to calm down, I'm the one that's poisoned. Mum doesn't even seem to care and is much more concerned about Trevor. Should I go to hospital?

Mum: Did you bring your glasses?

Trevor: Yes, of course I have. And spare contact lenses, so there's really no need to panic. (*Who's panicking?*)

Mum: Good, where are they? I'll fetch them for you.

Trevor: They're in my man bag which I gave to Ellie at the airport to carry onto the plane.

Me: No, you didn't.

Trevor: Yes, I did.

Me: Well, I didn't hear you.

Trevor: So are you telling me you left my man bag with my glasses and my spare contact lenses at the airport?

Me: No, I'm telling you, you never asked me to carry your bag for you.

Mum: Ellie, I can't believe you would do such a horrid thing!

Me: I didn't do anything. Why are you all blaming me?

Mum: Because you have deliberately been trying to sabotage (*great word, thanks Mum, I'd never have come up with that one on my own*) this holiday ever since we left Norbury.

Me: No, I haven't. *(Well, not much anyway).*

Trevor: Okay, let's all calm down everyone, I'll just have to manage with one contact lens.

Mum glared at me as Trevor put in his one lens and looked at us. Clearly the only way he could focus was by squinting with his other eye. It looked like he was permanently winking at us. Creepy.

Trevor: How's that?

Me: Um, yeah...looks fine.

Blue: TV! TV!

I was quite grateful for Blue's interruption as it distracted Mum and Trevor from what was potentially becoming a very ugly scene. We all turned to Blue, who was jumping up and down on the bed, waving a TV remote control in Trevor's face. Skye realised the implications of the find and joined in.

Skye: Pokemon! Pokemon!

Blue pressed a couple of buttons and a blast of cold air hit the back of my neck. I looked up. We all did.

Trevor (squinting)**:** That's an air conditioning unit, isn't it?

Great. I am totally dehydrated for nothing. If I am rushed to hospital and put on an emergency saline drip to replace the millions of vital mineral salts and gallons of liquid I have lost (*good knowledge of Biology to impress the examiner*), it will be all Trevor's fault. He should have known it was an AC unit. After all, he's the Geography teacher. The ventilation systems of foreign hotels must be on the syllabus, everything else is. That's it – I've had it with all of them.

TEXT FROM POPPY:

Home run!
Totally fantastic!

Great. On top of everything else, it's now official. I'm the only virgin in Year 11 and probably the only one in South London. The shame of it.

TEXT TO POPPY:

Shared room with
Mum etc. so nothing
doing this end.
I am soooooo
jealous.

TEXT FROM POPPY:

Totally selfish!
Don't give up.

12.00 noon – A pavement, somewhere in Greece.

I survived the ferry journey by sitting as far away as possible from anyone I know. The boat was full of old women dressed in black. Absolutely no talent whatsoever present on board.

Blue and Skye are now lobbing stones at the boats in the harbour. Mum is feeding the love child bright orange Cheetos as it has refused to eat everything else. Trevor is trying to hail a taxi. He has got a *Greek for Geeks* phrasebook in one hand and is currently shouting gibberish at anything with an engine.

12.15pm

The sun is scorching hot and Mum has just smothered us all in factor 50 suncream. We all look like mime artists; no wonder we can't get a lift.

12.30pm

Five taxis have ignored us so far.

Mum says it is because they probably think Trevor with his constant winking is trying to pick them up. That's right, blame it all on me.

1.00pm

Finally, a driver, unoffended by Trevor's advances, agrees to take us to a different pavement in a small town inland. Throughout the journey Trevor reads out various phrases from his book; sensibly the driver ignores him.

1.15pm

We appear to have arrived at a small village that has clearly been evacuated for some reason as there is not a soul in sight, apart from a mangy old dog tied up in a backyard which is barking madly at us and has obviously got rabies. I feel like Dorothy from the *Wizard of Oz* when she first finds herself in Oz and there's no one around (*although I wouldn't be seen dead in pigtails. Or a blue-checked dress. What was Aunty Em thinking?*)

Tiny, higgledy-piggledy shacks line the empty streets. (Higgledy-piggledy, *is that a word, or something made up for a nursery rhyme? Perhaps consider taking it out. Don't want to appear babyish, could cost me marks.*) It looks like one of those places they film for *Comic Relief*, to show in between the funny bits. (*Even though I obviously didn't wear a red nose I did buy one as I like to do my bit for charity.*)

Trevor has spent the last five minutes counting out the exact money for the taxi. The taxi driver looks less than impressed. As he leaves, he says something that sounds like 'malaka' so Trevor returns the compliment and says 'malaka' back.

Mum: What does *malaka* mean?

Trevor: Not sure, I'll have to check. I think it is used as a general greeting, like good day.

Mum: Well I'm really impressed; you seem to have picked up the language really quickly.

Trevor: Yes, it seems to come quite naturally to me. Right, where are we?

My thoughts exactly. Trevor has unfolded what looks like a paper napkin and is studying it closely.

Trevor: According to the directions, it's down here.

He is pointing down a narrow alleyway.

Mum: Are you sure?

Trevor: Elaine, I *am* a Geography teacher.

2.00pm

Oh my God! Trevor's booked us into a hovel.

We traipsed behind Trevor for ages until suddenly he stopped and pointed to a hut with a tin roof. I dropped my bags onto the dusty road and stood open-mouthed, which is a very unattractive look, I know. The street looked like the aftermath of an earthquake. I couldn't contain myself any longer.

Me: Tell me we aren't staying here. It's a hovel!

Mum: Ellie!

Me: Well, it is – it's awful, Mum. Surely you don't like it?

I appealed to Mum. Surely she would agree with me and demand that Trevor either sorted something else out immediately or we would check into the nearest Hilton Hotel. The village was a ghost town. No nail bars, no Monsoon, no Ravel. You simply can't survive those conditions (*not that those are the only things I'm interested in, Mr Examiner. There don't seem to be any art galleries or museums either*). And as for our accommodation, Norbury train station has got more appeal than this.

Mum: Actually, I love it. I think it's charming.

Me: You can't be serious. Cardboard city has got more charm than that.

Mum: Let's take a look inside before we go jumping to any conclusions, shall we?

Me: What do you think it is? A Tardis? It'll be just as bad inside.

Mum: Stop it Ellie! You're causing a scene.

Me: No Mum, to cause a scene you need an audience. There's just us in this horrible ghost town of a place.

Mum: And them.

She nodded over my shoulder. I turned around. On the opposite side of the road, sitting outside a hovel identical to ours were two little old people perched on stools. They looked like a couple of wrinkled old gnomes. They watched us intently, then nodded at Trevor. Trevor waved and called over to them.

Trevor: Malaka!

Mum smiled.

Mum: Malaka! Ooh, look at me I'm speaking Greek!

The couple looked at each other and frowned.

Mum: Now Ellie, let's go inside and sort this out.

Surprise, surprise, I was right: the inside is just as bad. There's a pokey little kitchen with a grimy sink, a small fridge and a wobbly table. Leading off the kitchen are three rooms. Each has two put-me-ups in them. Honestly, I'd prefer it if someone *put-me-down*. I dumped my stuff on one of the beds and then realised something was missing.

Me: Where's the bathroom?

Mum: I'm not sure. Trevor, where's the bathroom?

Trevor: I think it's out the back. You'll have to go out the front door and walk around the side of the house.

I decided to go out and investigate but I couldn't see anything that looked remotely like a toilet so I went back inside.

Me: Nope, there's nothing but an old shed.

Mum: Oh dear, that's not good.

At last, I was getting somewhere. There was no way Mum was going stay in a place with no en-suite bathroom. No need to unpack.

Me: Perhaps we should just cut our losses and check into a hotel?

Mum: Well...

Trevor: Did you check the shed?

Me: Yes, but there was no toilet in it.

Trevor: Let's go and see.

So Trevor and I went out together. We stood in the doorway of the shed.

Trevor: Thought so.

He looked down at our feet where there was a hole in the ground and then turned and winked at me which, to be honest, is beginning to freak me out.

Trevor: It's Turkish.

Me: I thought we were in Greece – and can you try not to wink at me?

Trevor: No, Turkish is the type of toilet that has a hole in the ground. You place your feet either side of the hole and squat down over the hole.

Me: Too much information. I can't possibly do that.

Trevor: You don't have much choice.

Me: I hate you.

Trevor: I know.

I marched back into the house and to my room. I could hear Trevor explaining the toilet arrangements. Mum just gave a nervous laugh and said she hoped her aim was up to it. How repulsive.

2.15pm

I'm desperate to go to the toilet, but there's no way I'm using that vile contraption (*two good words there. Also got to be some kind of illegal hygiene issues here – another reason for the examiner to alert the authorities*). Trevor has apparently left to get 'provisions'.

2.30pm

I'm still bursting for a wee and I'm starving.

2.45pm

Trevor's back. Let's hope he managed to get some kebabs.

2.50pm

Trevor's 'provisions' consist of a ruler ('I was trying to buy stamps'), a tomato ('I asked for five') and a box of tissues ('I thought I had asked for sandwiches').

Mum: What happened to the kebabs?

I could tell Mum wasn't impressed. It's about time she saw through him.

Trevor: It's not as easy as you think, Elaine. All I could find was a man sitting in a kiosk. He didn't speak any English. I had to shout through a tiny little window, plus it doesn't help when you've only got one good eye. He kept looking at me very strangely. I think he thought I was trying to chat him up or something.

Gross.

3.00pm

I'm desperate. I'm going to have to go and use the shed.

3.05pm

Fairly certain I'm now traumatised for life.

I can't bear to write about it, in case it causes secondary trauma *(I know all about that from Holby City)*. Years from now, it will all spill out during a therapy session and be identified as the starting point for my emotional turmoil and inability to form lasting relationships with members of the opposite sex. If I never get married, it will be all Trevor's fault. And I really am starving.

3.10pm

Trevor has suggested we catch a bus to a nearby beach to try and find a restaurant, or taverna as they are called in Greece. Mum wanted to hire a car but Trevor has refused on the grounds that it is unnecessary and unnecessary car journeys are polluting the environment. The man eats so many green lentils that he's doing a pretty good job of that himself.

4.00pm

On the beach with the 'others'. At least there are some other people here. Maybe some fit guys will turn up.

Me: What are you wearing?

Mum: What?

Me: What are you wearing?

I am staring at Mum's knitted bathing costume. It looks like it has been dyed in a puddle.

Mum: Trevor bought it for me. It's untreated sheep's wool.

Me: You can't wear a bathing costume made of wool. It'll sag.

Trevor: It's not just any wool. It comes from the *Blue du Maine* sheep farmed by the Co-operative Rural Agricultural Project in the

Outer Hebrides. Look, here's the label.

Me: CRAP?

Mum: Ellie, that's not necessary.

Me: I can still see bits of grass in it. Doesn't it itch?

Mum: A bit.

Trevor: A small price to pay to save a centuries-old tradition, I think.

4.30pm

Trevor and his savages have gone rock-pooling. Love child is asleep and Mum is pretending to read *A Suitable Boy*.

I feel like a mutant. Everyone else on the beach is a gorgeous bronze colour and looks fabulous in their bikini (*apart from Mum, who looks like Wilma out of the Flintstones*) whereas I, with my red hair and sheet-white body, resemble a lollipop. I can't risk getting up and going into the sea, someone might see me and call a doctor. I'll have to stay here under my towel.

4.45pm

Oh, God. Mum has just tried to persuade me that Trevor is human.

Mum: You don't like him much, do you?

Me: It's not that I don't like him (*lie*), it's just that I don't understand what you see in him. He's so geeky and not a patch on Dad.

Mum: Ellie, you need to understand that there's no possibility of your dad and I getting back together. You need to accept that.

Me: I have accepted it. And please don't tell me I am in denial, I'm not.

I know all about denial from Poppy who learnt about it from *Sugarscape.com*, although it took a while to get the gist of it.

Poppy: It's like you're in denial about your parents splitting up.

Me: No I'm not. I've never denied that my parents are divorced.

Poppy: No, denial means you haven't really accepted the situation. Your head knows your parents have split up, but your heart hasn't really come to terms with it.

Me: Yes, it has. I just don't think they made the right decision.

Poppy: See.

Me: No.

Poppy: Now you're denying you're in denial. That's just stupid.

Mum: I'm not suggesting you're in denial, Ellie. I just think that in your eyes no one will be able to fill your dad's shoes and that's fine, but in my case, he's not such a hard act to follow.

Me: Go on then.

Mum: What?

Me: Tell me, what's so special about Trevor?

Mum: Okay, if you really want to know, Trevor has, well he's opened my eyes to life's possibilities. For him life isn't about making money or climbing the career ladder. It's about growing as an individual. Life's an experience, to be marvelled at and appreciated. (*Oh God, sounds like something out of my PSHE lessons. In a minute, she'll be telling me about 'life's rich tapestry' and that 'life's what you make it'*). You see, Ellie, I want to look beyond Danielle Steel, *Marie Claire* and Toni and Guy. I want to discover the real world. Is that such a bad thing?

Me: You could've done that with Dad.

Mum: No, that's just the point, I couldn't. Your dad sees life as one big business opportunity. If he were here now he wouldn't be messing around in rock pools looking for hermit crabs like Trevor is, he'd be on his mobile chasing another get-rich-quick scheme that always meant we ended up poorer-even-sooner.

Me: At least he's exciting. You never know what he's going to do next. Trevor is so...dull.

Mum: The trouble with excitement, Ellie, is it's a bit like a boy band – short-lived and very overrated. Now, are you coming for a swim?

That's *so* not true. Westlife are amazing *and* have been around forever.

Me: No.

Mum: Suit yourself.

I watched her as she joined the 'unit' who were inspecting some sea creature among the rocks. She knelt down beside them and laughed as they terrorised some poor unsuspecting sea aneno...amenon...creature.

My eyes began to sting a bit, probably the salt in the air. No Mum, if I was suiting myself I would be sitting at a poolside bar with Dad and Delph sipping Barcadi Breezers (*okay, perhaps that's taking it a bit far – besides, don't want the examiner reporting me for underage drinking*) and mulling over which pair of pumps would go best with my evening outfit that I'd just bought from Chloé.

It's the first time Mum has spoken about Dad like that before. My parents' break-up has always been a conversational no-go area. At the time, they were both so intent on telling me how much they loved me and that I wasn't in any way responsible for them splitting up. This was ironic. (*At least I think it was – check with Miss B – I'm not too clear on irony. We did it last year when we did Shakespeare's* Othello. *Apparently Othello, who sounded well fit, is being ironic when he says to Desdemona 'Honey, you will be desired in Cyprus,' because what he really means is she is going to be bumped off. I didn't get it at all. I just thought 'lucky cow, you've got a gorgeous husband and an entire island fancies you.' Perhaps I should've gone to Cyprus. In the end, Miss B got fed up with us being so dim and said, 'it's just like sarcasm'. Why didn't she say that in the first place? Everyone knows what sarcasm means. Duh!*)

Anyway, it seemed ironic that Mum and Dad kept saying, 'Ellie, you are the innocent party in all of this' as I hadn't thought of blaming myself at all until they mentioned it. The result was that they completely forgot to tell me the reason why they didn't want to be married to each other anymore.

I was eleven at the time and to be honest I don't remember a great deal of drama. It happened very quickly and very quietly. If it weren't for the fact that Dad wasn't there in the evenings anymore I probably wouldn't have noticed.

There were no screaming matches, no tantrums, no recriminations (*great word, that has to be A-level standard*). One day Dad was there, the next day he was gone. Poppy said it wasn't natural; her dad's break-ups were accompanied by lots of shouting and huge crockery bills. She said that my parents had 'internalised' their grief at their marriage ending and that it would all come out some day.

Poppy: Your mother will probably have a nervous breakdown, spend ten years on Prozac and then get herself a girlfriend. Your dad will just become an alcoholic and end up living on the streets, selling the *Big Issue*.

How embarrassing would that be? Coming out of Norbury station to find your dad trying to flog you the *Big Issue*. But life carried on as normal – too normal. Dad continued to be Dad; the only thing that changed was that he became a 'weekend father' and I would go and stay with him in his bedsit in Peckham. (*Peckham?! What is it with divorcees? Their property judgement goes completely out the window!*) It was a bit weird being on my own with him at first and we spent a lot of time watching *Match of the Day*, but it gave me the opportunity to mark the bottles in his drinks cabinet. Mum also seemed to carry on as if nothing had happened and her bedside cabinet contained nothing stronger than Oil of Evening Primrose and St John's Wort.

Today is the closest she's ever come to telling me what drove them apart and the fact that it is because Dad is just too exciting doesn't strike me as a good enough reason to leave someone.

TEXT FROM POPPY:

Dumped chef.
Didn't have a car.
Found any Greek
Gods?

Oh God, that's all I need, pressure from Poppy. The only Greeks I

58

have seen at close quarters are the two toothless crinklies who live opposite us on 'Earthquake Street'.

TEXT TO POPPY:

Mum won't let me out
of her sight.

TEXT FROM POPPY:

That's disgraceful.
Get yourself taken into care.
They're allowed to do anything.
Keep me informed.

I'm not going to be able to stall Poppy for much longer. I'll have to find a boyfriend and soon. I'll cast an eye around the beach. If there are any lush guys to be found, it *has* to be on the beach.

Well, that was a total waste of time. The beach is shaped like a horse-shoe and edged with tavernas. It's fairly deserted, with just a couple of families splashing about in the sea but little else. The only other young people are a couple sunbathing about twenty metres away. The girl is stretched out on her front on a sunbed and looks stunning in a lime green bikini. Her head is tilted towards me and her dark hair is hanging over the edge of the bed. She looks – what's the word – sultry (*fabulous word! Higher grade at GCSE, here I come*). God, what I wouldn't give to look sultry! I'd even settle for vaguely appealing.

At the last school disco, Poppy and I spent the afternoon in front of my bedroom mirror, practicing looking sexy. Poppy smouldered, of course. I just came off as sullen (*again – wow, these words are just pouring out!*). In the car on the way to the disco Mum asked if I'd hurt myself as I was wearing the same look as just after I had my TB jab. An expression of acute pain was the only thing I pulled that night. I left early and Poppy bagged herself Ben Hardy, a sixth-former!! How does she do it? (*Though of course they only kissed – wouldn't want to get Ben in trouble with the police*).

The girl's companion, her boyfriend I assume, looks a total and utter geek, so it's not all bad. What is it with women who are attracted to nerdy blokes? He's sitting on the edge of the sunbed, blowing up an inflatable crocodile. He's so skinny; his bones are sticking out of his shoulders. He has a thick mop of black hair which he has made no attempt to style or anything. Oh no, how embarrassing! He has just shifted his weight and the sunbed has flipped up, depositing him on the sand. How excruciating, but he's just grinning like an idiot. Even his girlfriend finds it funny. I'd have dumped him immediately. He has now picked up the crocodile and run into the sea with it. I'm surprised he has the strength.

The situation is getting serious. My chances of meeting a decent guy are nil. I wish I'd gone to Italy. They're obviously falling over themselves to go out with Poppy. If I don't get off with a boy soon, I'll never be able to show my face in school ever again. I'll be an outcast. Maybe I should mention the benefits of homeschooling to Mum.

A sleepover at Poppy's recently revealed that most of the girls in my class have done it, even speccy Susan, who's morphed into some kind of sex siren after ditching her specs for some cobalt-blue contact lenses. If I don't get my act together Poppy will go off with Susan and swap 'what's it like'-type stories with her. I can hear Poppy's voice now:

Poppy: Elles, I'd love you to come to town with us, but you simply wouldn't understand the conversation.

Oh God, Lucy Telling with her yellow teeth will become my best friend, my only friend. God, I am bursting for a pee. I'm off to see if I can find some 'English' toilets.

5.15pm

Wow, I have just seen the hunkiest guy ever in the history of the universe!

He's sitting in a taverna. He's wearing a tight white T-shirt, tight black trousers and has slicked back hair. Great bum. Looks a bit like that cute guy out of *Glee*, the football player. I reckon he's at least seventeen. I think he's noticed me too, either that or he was just showing concern for my whiteness. It's difficult to tell the difference.

5.25pm

Omigod, the bloke from the taverna has just laid his towel down near mine.

He has taken his shirt off and he is toooootally gorgeous! His chest is all smooth and shiny. He looks like an extra for that dance group women hire for their hen nights, the Chippendales – although Poppy says they are all gay and the women who go along to smear baby oil all over them and grab their pants are just deluding themselves.

5.30pm

Omigod, he's smiling at me – I think. Actually, he could just be squinting.

5.35pm

Must share the news!

TEXT TO POPPY:

Just met total
Greek God.
Definitely a ten

Okay, technically we haven't met – yet.

TEXT FROM POPPY:

Go for it. Maitre d' has
asked for my room number!
Definitely an 11.

It sounds like Poppy has set her sights high. At the moment, I'd be happy with the kitchen boy.

5.40pm

OMG, he's just spoken to me. I must try to remember exactly what he said.

Greek God: Are you cold?

Me: No, why?

The Greek God points to the beach towel that is covering my entire body up to my neck.

Me: Right. The sun. Hot. I burn easily.

Greek God: Yes. The baby? Ees yours?

Me: Baby? Oh, that baby. God, no chance! It's a right pain – cries all the time.

Greek God: Me, I love keeds.

Me: So do I. Hope to have lots myself one day.

Silence...

5.45pm

Aaaaaaaaargh!

Trevor has ruined everything. I hate him more than I hate the

Sugababes. He just came back from the sea and plonked himself down between me and the Greek God. How insensitive can you be?

Trevor: Have a bash at this one, Ellie. Which city-state known for its harsh way of life began on the Peloponnese?

I know who I'd like to bash.

Me: Kabul. (*Oh God, now the Greek God thinks I am really thick, but I can't let Trevor think his little tests are working. It would make him insufferable – wow, a four syllable word, I didn't even look it up in a thesaurus so beat that, Clarissa-smart-arse-straight-A's-Dobson!*)

Trevor: No, it's Sparta. You know, as in the adjective, spartan.

Me: Right.

Then, as if it couldn't get any worse, Trevor actually looked across at the Greek God, nodded at him and then turned to me.

Trevor: He's a bit buff, isn't he?

I was speechless:

   a) no one uses words like buff and

   b) Trevor has killed any chances I have of getting off with anyone at all. Ever.

Trevor: Anyway, your mum and I thought we would grab a bite to eat. Coming?

Me: No, I'm not hungry, thanks.

Trevor: Suit yourself.

No Trevor, if I was suiting myself you would dissolve into the sand and I would be in the arms of the Adonis sat next to me (*good to show the examiner I'm familiar with Classics. Actually I picked it up from a quiz on Sugarscape.com:* Is your bloke an arse or an Adonis? *I should've let Mum do the quiz, it might've been the wake up call she needs.*)

Just then, Mum returned with the evil twins. She took one look at the Greek God and instantly put him in the frame for the Norbury rapes.

Mum: Who's that?

Me: Dunno. Stop scowling at him.

Mum: Well, why's he sat so close to us?

Me: Dunno. It's a public beach, he can sit where he likes.

Mum: Right, well, we're all going for something to eat.

Me: I'm not, I'm staying here.

Mum glared at the Greek God. Perhaps she was considering a citizen's arrest.

Mum: I don't think so, young lady.

Me: But I'm not hungry.

Trevor: Elaine, Elaine, she'll be fine. If we sit outside the taverna, we'll be able to see her.

Creep! His feeble attempts to get round me are totally wasted. I can see right through him. Mum rummaged around in her beach bag.

Mum: Okay Ellie, but take this.

Me: Hairspray?

Mum shook the can vigorously and handed it to me. She stared at the gorgeous guy sitting just yards away but he just looked out to sea.

Mum: Anyone bothers you, just point it in their face and press down hard.

Trevor: D'you know how much damage those things do to the environment?

Mum: My daughter's safety is more important than the ozone layer, Trevor.

Blue: Can I have some hairspray?

6.00ρm – Sitting on the beach, alone.

The 'unit' finally left me alone and went to a taverna, but I've blown my chances of ever getting a boyfriend. I can't even blame this one on Trevor. And, believe me, I've tried.

Just after the others left, the Greek God spoke to me again. He jerked his head in the direction of 'unit', who were disappearing down the beach.

GG (Greek God)**:** Your father?

Me: No, of course not.

GG: Your boyfriend?

Me: Yuk, no.

GG frowned.

GG: He like men?

Me: Um, I don't think so.

GG: He wink at me many times.

Me: Oh right. No, eye problem. He's my mother's, er, boyfriend.

GG: Good.

Me: No, not really. In fact, very bad.

GG: You no like.

Me: I no like.

Then the conversation petered out, which was just as well as I needed time to digest what had just taken place. First of all, he started the conversation. That could mean:

a) he fancies me

b) he's bored

c) he's checking I am still conscious.

Re his questions about Trevor: surely that was to check that I'm available, although I felt a bit insulted that he thought I would go out with an old hippy who wears cut-off denim jeans for swimming shorts. On the other hand he could be worried that Trevor might beat him up if he tried it on with me. No worries there, Trevor couldn't beat an egg. If there's any violence, it's more likely to come from Mum. So what did it all mean? Did he fancy me or not? Where was Poppy when I needed her? She would know what to do. I texted her whole conversation; she replied immediately.

TEXT FROM POPPY:

He is so into you,
Elles. Go for it.

Great, trust Poppy to know what to do. I steeled myself to speak to the Greek God. I rehearsed what I was going to say and glanced across at him. His towel was vacant. I looked out to sea just in time to see him disappear into the surf.

Oh God, what did that mean? Did he want me to follow him? Or wait here until he got out? Perhaps he got bored while I was texting Poppy and gave up. Oh no! Perhaps he thought I wasn't interested. I'll have to text Poppy for some more advice.

Suddenly I heard squeals and screams, followed by shouting. Great, the rabble were returning. I'd totally screwed up.

Skye: Ellie! Ellie! We ate octopus.

Me: Really, did you wait until they killed it?

Mum: Ellie!

Trevor: We brought you back a kebab, in case you're hungry.

Me: No, ta.

My mum might be an easy touch, but I'm not. You can't worm your way into my affections like you have with her. Loser.

Trevor: Right, I've got a good one for you. What is the small landlocked country between Spain and France?

Me: Angola.

Trevor: Almost, you got the 'An' bit right. It's Andorra.

68

9.00pm

I'm sitting in my cell back at the hovel and I am famished, totally ravenous (*two adjectives in one sentence! Not bad considering I'm weak with hunger*). We returned to the hovel two hours ago and all I've had to eat is a tomato and a raw courgette. Trevor is teaching the 'unit' to play gin rummy, although the love child is more interested in eating the cards and Blue is too busy drawing boobs on the queens.

9.30pm

It's no good, I'm going to have to eat.

10.30pm

Wow, well that was totally worth it – once I got past the camp guards.

Me: I'm hungry, I'm going to see if there's anywhere to get some food.

Mum: Hang on, I'll come with you. You don't know who's out there.

Me: No, Mum, I'd rather go on my own. This isn't Brixton.

Trevor: Elaine, Ellie's fifteen, she's lived all her life in London, she'll be fine.

Mum: Okay, but take the Silvikrin and keep the nozzle facing forwards.

I wandered into the village square holding the hairspray. It was quite late, but the place was buzzing with people. OMG, where did they all come from? And where do they all go during the day? Perhaps they only come out at night because they're all vampires. I kept an eye out for an Edward Cullen look-alike. Now *that* would've been totally cool.

Outside a cafe, a bunch of old men were laughing and arguing over a game of backgammon. A couple of little kids were speeding around the paved square on tricycles while a group of youths sat by a fountain, admiring each other's mopeds. I walked around the edge of the square, avoiding them at all costs. It's bad enough having to walk past English boys; I couldn't bear walking past boys speaking a foreign language.

On the far side of the square I spotted a large kiosk. Next to it, on a rack were some large bags of crisps. That'll do, I thought. I quickly walked over, head bowed. There was no one at the kiosk so I picked up three bags of Cheetos and placed them on the counter. I wondered if I should say 'malaka' to the guy behind the counter but he would probably laugh and tell everyone in the square so I just handed over a 10 euro note. He gave me the change and I gathered up the Cheetos. When I turned around, a familiar face was smiling at me.

GG: Hello.

Me: Hello.

I was so shocked, I dropped the can of hairspray and ran off. My heart was racing out of control. Back at the hovel I returned to my cell to reflect on what had just happened.

He said hello; what could that mean? It could be:

a) he still fancies me or

b) he was buying his own Cheetos, or

c) it doesn't matter now as I just ran off without saying anything.

Why does life always have to be so complicated? Every time I replay my meeting with the Greek God, my stomach turns over and my heart begins to pound. Is this what love feels like?

DAY THREE

11.00am

I've hardly slept a wink.

I keep mulling over what the Greek God meant exactly when he said hello to me last night in the kiosk queue. I wish Poppy was here. She would know precisely what to do, but I can't text her because she'll also know I haven't got anywhere near 'doing it'.

12.30pm

After trying to leave the hovel for the last three hours we have finally made it to the beach. Mum went into a bit of a panic when she put on her woollen bathing costume and realized it had started to unravel.

Mum: One of my buttocks is poking through. (*Yuk, that's so gross!*)

She was all for buying a new one before Trevor gave her a needle and thread he happened to have brought with him so she could fix it. For a minute she didn't seem to know what to do with it. (*I'd have stabbed him with it, personally.*) Then Trevor couldn't get his contact lens in: 'it's virtually disintegrated' (*drama queen, although disintegrated is a great word*) and the evil twins wanted to bury a dead lizard they had found so they could make their own fossil.

(*Why bother? You already have one. He's called Trevor.*)

On arrival at the beach, I quickly sweep the area for evidence of the Greek God, but he's not here which leaves me feeling flat. I notice the nerd and his girlfriend that were here yesterday are back again. Her long, syrupy limbs are draped over a sun bed. I never thought I could feel so much hate for someone I don't even know. Her geek's face is buried in a book. What does she see in him?

Mum is massaging suncream into Trevor's back which is quite disgusting. The love child is eating the sand, which probably tastes as good as the Cheetos. Blue and Skye are tracking the progress of a giant ant.

Me: I'm bored.

Mum: Go for a swim.

Trevor: This one'll interest you, Ellie. What is the largest Japanese island?

Me: Obi-Wan Kenobi?

Trevor: I don't think I know that one. Anyway, it's Honshu, or Hondo. Actually, it's a bit of a trick question because it's the Japanese mainland, which is also an island.

Me: Right.

Mum: Why don't you build a sandcastle?

Me: Mum, I'm nearly sixteen; I haven't built a sandcastle since I was six. I'm not a kid.

Blue: Yes, yes, Ellie build a sandcastle.

Me: No.

12.45pm

Still no sign of the Greek God. Hmmm, he said he liked little kids, bizarrely. Perhaps if he turned up and saw me playing lovingly with the savages, he would like me even more.

Me: I have an idea, why don't you bury me in sand up to my knees.

Mum: Thanks Ellie.

Trevor: Yeah, that's a really cool offer.

Cool? What a jerk! I'm not doing it for you, mum-stealer. Hopefully, the evil twins won't have reached my ankles by the time GG arrives and then I can make my excuses and get shot of them.

1.00pm

The savages are heaping sand on me with worrying enthusiasm. I may have to stop writing.

2.00pm

Those nasty, vile, evil, vicious kids. I hate them.
  I'm still trying to remove sand from every crevice in my body.

The little misfits covered me from head to foot in gritty sand. What was worse, Mum and Trevor just smiled at them indulgently (*great word, shame I had to use it in this context, but it's true, they never seem to indulge* me) as they buried me alive.

When I was totally submerged under the sand, the little sods shoved a couple of Cheetos up my nose. Then out of the corner of my eye I spotted the Greek God sauntering along the beach, heading in my direction. Oh no! Disaster, I couldn't let him see me like this. I decided the best course of action was to pretend to be asleep. It didn't work.

Greek God: Hi again.

I opened one eye.

Me: Di.

The Greek God frowned and headed off towards the geek and his girlfriend at the other end of the bay. He probably fancies her more than me anyway.

Mum watched him leave, her eyes narrowed.

Mum: What did that boy mean by 'again'?

Me: Dunno.

Mum: He definitely said 'hi again'. Have you met him before somewhere?

Me: No.

Mum continued to stare at him. My heart sank. Mum never forgets a face, especially any that show any interest in me. After all, this is the woman who's tried to ban me from Facebook (*'a hunting ground for psychopaths'. I'm not even allowed membership to Club*

Penguin.) Of course, I have an account anyway, but it's under the name Nellie Boster (*clever alias I know. May have to delete as don't want the examiner thinking I always ignore parental orders.*)

Mum: He was on the beach yesterday, wasn't he?

Me: No.

Mum: Don't lie to me, young lady. I know he was. I don't want you talking to him, he's far too old for you.

According to my mum, anyone who is more than a month older than me is 'too old' and if they are more than six months older than me then they are 'nothing better than a paedophile, preying on innocent young girls'. But as I wouldn't be seen dead with a younger boy (*so immature*), my options are limited. The only boy I know who is fifteen years and ten months old is Geoffrey Speakman who, it has to be said, is quite good-looking but Poppy says he's far too hygenic to be heterosexual and is almost certainly gay, he just doesn't know it yet.

2.30pm

Oh no, the Greek God is chatting to the nerd and his girlfriend.

She'll probably ditch that idiot boyfriend of hers and go out with him now. He's even sitting on the edge of her sunbed stroking her arm and her boyfriend isn't doing a thing to stop him. The Greek God hasn't looked in my direction once. He has completely forgotten I ever existed.

☆ ☆ ☆ ☆ ☆

3.00pm

Fantastic news: help is finally on its way. Mum's relationship with Trevor is destined for trouble...

After my ordeal at the hands of the Satan's offspring, I decided to join the 'unit' for lunch. We sat down at a table and Trevor immediately got out his phrasebook.

Trevor: I wonder what the Greek for mung beans is.

He insisted on ordering everything in Greek, even though the waiter told him he'd spent three years studying politics at Middlesex University. When he'd finally finished, the waiter mumbled 'malaka' and disappeared into the kitchen.

Trevor: You know, I'm not sure *malaka* does mean 'good morning'. Perhaps it means 'well done' but I can't find it anywhere in my book.

Mum: I think it's really brave to try and learn a new language. I can't speak of word of anything, apart from English – and I'm not great at that.

Trevor squeezed Mum's hand. Repulsive.

Trevor: Oh it's nothing really, just a matter of confidence.

Mum: Ellie, you should give it a whirl. You're good at French. You might find you're a natural like Trevor.

Trevor: Ah, parles-tu français?

Me: Non.

At last the food arrived. The savages ignored the vegetarian option of Greek salad that Trevor had ordered for them and when he wasn't looking grabbed a handful of my kebabs. Even the love child traded some Cheetos for a spoonful of moussaka. Just as we finished, a phone went off. I thought it might be an urgent call from Poppy, but then I realised it couldn't be my phone. I wouldn't be seen dead with *Dancing Queen* for my ringtone. It was Mum's phone. She retrieved it from her handbag and checked the screen. It was a text. Her face fell.

Mum: Oh no, it's GM.

Trevor frowned, stabbing a cucumber with his fork and studying it intently with his one eye.

Trevor: Hardly, Elaine. The Greeks pride themselves on using natural ingredients. The food isn't technically organic as they don't belong to The Soil Association, but it's certainly not genetically modified.

Mum: No, no not GM, *GM*.

I glanced up.

Me: Grandma?

Mum's face clouded over.

Mum: Yes, Grandma.

Trevor: Oh no. What does she want?

Mum: She's thinking of coming here.

Me: Great!

At last, reinforcements! My grandmother insists on being called GM, because she says Grandma 'makes me sound old before my time'. Her real name is Ida, so she has a point. But best of all, she hates Trevor, or 'that pompous arse', as she calls him. Actually, she hates Dad too, who she calls 'that arrogant arse' but that's another story.

Trevor: I thought she was trekking in the Amazon.

Mum: Cancelled apparently, due to heavy rain.

Trevor: What does she expect? It's a rainforest, for God's sake!

Me: When's she coming?

Mum: She's not sure. Depends if she can get a cheap flight or not.

The mood around the table plummeted. My mum chased a chunk of tomato around her plate in a desultory fashion (*desultory! Best word yet! Beat that, Clarissa-hand-your-coursework-in-early Dobson!*) Trevor leafed through his phrasebook, looking for the Greek for tofu. The love child, sensing something was up, started shaking. The savages played sword-fighting with the kebab sticks.

I, on the other hand, was jubilant, of course. Inside, I was leaping for joy at the thought of GM coming to sort this mess out. GM will succeed where I have failed. She will break the spell Trevor holds over my Mum.

Mum sighed heavily.

Mum: Well, let's not let it spoil our meal.

But it already had. Mum and GM don't really see eye to eye.

Mum's always complaining about GM's behaviour. According to her, GM went 'off the rails' after Granddad died (*before I was born*), which is a bit rich considering Mum is a divorced single mother shacked up with a hippy (*on weekends and Wednesdays*) and their love child. GM says she's just making up for lost time. At least she knows how to have fun.

GM: I wasn't even a foot soldier when the sexual revolution happened. Now, I intend to be Che-bloody-Guevara.

I've no idea who she was talking about (*should find out and include, to demonstrate historical knowledge*), but it's fair to say that she has had a string of men or 'lovers', as she insists on calling them (*'darling, boyfriend is such a dull word. It lacks passion, something I don't'*). Personally, I don't mind GM's behaviour. She can do what she likes, just as long as she continues to hate Trevor as much as I do.

4.15pm – **Back on the beach.**

The gorgeous Greek God is messing about in the sea with the nerd's girlfriend. They're splashing each other – so immature. Wish it was me. The nerd is asleep; can't he see the Greek God is stealing his girlfriend from right under his nose? I've got a good mind to go over and tell him. Hey, you gotta fight, fight, fight, fight, fight for your love in this world (*Cheryl Cole – what a Goddess. Can't believe Ashley cheated on her*).

TEXT FROM POPPY:

I've done 'it' twice already.

Great, isn't it?
Don't spare the details.

Oh no, that's all I needed. What did she mean by 'details'?

TEXT TO POPPY:

Totally!
No time now,
will tell all later.

Tell what? Swapping hellos under my mother's prison-warden stare hardly counts as a sexual experience.
  Oh no, Trevor is looking at me.

Trevor: Right, Ellie, name one other country that has a rainforest.

Me: Egypt.

Trevor: Er, no, I don't think so. You know, if you're planning to do A-level Geography, you might have to think about improving your general knowledge.

Me: Right.

6.00pm – Back at the hovel.

I've got to get out of here. Trevor and Mum can't keep their hands off each other – it's nauseating. Still, they may as well make the most of it. If GM shows up, it'll be curtains for them. The savages are outside persecuting the local wildlife.

Me: I thought I'd wander into the village and buy something to eat.

Mum: I'll come with you.

Trevor: I'm sure Ellie can manage alone, Elaine. I was – er, thinking of taking a short siesta. You know, 'when in Rome'.

He looks at Mum through half-closed eyes. I think he was aiming for seductive, but he just looks like he's partially-sighted. It's taking all my strength not to vomit.

Mum: Actually, I *am* a bit tired. I think I've had a bit too much sun. Don't be long, Ellie.

☆ ☆ ☆ ☆ ☆

6.45pm

Wow, am I glad I did that!...

I've just returned from the village, where I went to the kiosk and bought some more Cheetos, four cans of Amstel lager, some sunflower seeds and a Mars ice cream. (*See, Trevor, it's not that difficult. Ok, I was actually after 4 Bacardi Breezers, a sandwich and some Pringles but I got pretty close.*)
  I was in no hurry to return to the love nest so I decided to sit on the low wall next to the kiosk and eat my ice cream. There were a few people milling around, but no sign of the Greek God. I finished my ice cream and, whilst thinking about whether I actually wanted to drink the beer, started to text Poppy.

TEXT TO POPPY:

Greek God totally lush.
Great bod.

GG: Hi!

I recognized his voice instantly and glanced up. There he was, watching over me, amusement twinkling in his honey-coloured eyes. My very own Greek God. With the sun behind him, he looked like some kind of heavenly vision, an angel come to save me from my family and other hangers on.

I snapped my phone shut in case he saw what I had written to Poppy.

Me: Hi.

Brilliantly delivered, even if I say so myself. Friendly, but not too friendly and with just the hint of a smile. Poppy would be proud of me.

Greek God: You like Cheetos?

He nodded at the three huge bags of crisps on the wall next to me.

Me: Not really. They're for the love- er, the baby.

GG: You good sister.

Me: Yes, I suppose I am (*lie*).

GG: You like Greece.

Me: Love it (*another lie*).

GG: Eets land of the Gods.

Me: Absolutely.

GG: You like Greek men?

Oh God, it was all going so well. I had no idea what to say? If I said yes, I could sound too forward. If I said no, I might put him off altogether.

Me: Some.

Totally brilliant, Ellie. Right, GG, pick the bones out of that. He looked at the cans of lager. I nonchalantly (*great word*) cracked open a can and took a big swig, immediately bursting into a coughing/choking fit as the bubbles went up my nose. It tasted disgusting.

GG: You drink beer a lot.

Me: All the time.

GG: I see you on beach tomorrow.

Christ! (*Perhaps I shouldn't take the Lord's name in vain, examiner may be religious.*) Was he telling me to be on the beach tomorrow? I had no idea; I decided to just smile sweetly.

The Greek God returned the smile and wandered off to join a group of boys on the other side of the square.

Wow, that's definitely a date, I think. I floated back to the hovel, dumping the remaining cans of beer in the bin on the way. My head is spinning. I have never felt this happy. I can't wait until tomorrow. I texted Poppy immediately.

TEXT TO POPPY:

Have date with

Greek God.

TEXT FROM POPPY:

Lucky cow!
Maitre d'
married.
It's off.

Even Poppy has her standards.

I reached the hovel to find Mum sitting outside alone 'soaking up the atmosphere'.

Mum: The rhythmic chants of the cicadas are so soothing, don't you think?

Me: That and ten Benson and Hedges.

Mum: There's no need for that. You've been a while.

Me: Big queue at the kiosk. Thought if I didn't get the love child some more Cheetos we'd be up the spout without a paddle.

Mum: Don't mix your metaphors. It's up the creek without a paddle and you're right, we're clean out of Cheetos. (*Will leave that bit in. Surely mixed metaphors are worth more marks as it shows originality.*)

11.00pm

Can't sleep, I'm so excited about tomorrow. I can hear the savages next door, probably tormenting some poor gecko.

11.25pm

With my ear pressed against the wall I can hear the evil twins talking and I'm appalled. *(Good word, Mrs Duce uses it all the time, as in: 'I'm appalled at your inability to grasp basic biological concepts such as photosynthesis.' I have grasped it, Mrs Duce, I'm just not interested in the eating habits of weeds.)*

Blue: Do you think Elaine will become our Mummy? I don't want a new Mummy.

Skye: No way, José.

Blue: But Trevor says he loves her. Why?

Skye: I don't know. She's a cow.

Blue: She hates us because we're not her children.

Skye: If we behave, maybe Trevor will leave her.

Blue: Maybe, and she'll take that horrible Ellie with her.

Skye: I hate Ellie.

Blue: Smelly Ellie!

Skye: Haha. It was funny when we stuck those Cheetos up her nose. She was really cross.

The two of them dissolve into a fit of giggles. What a cheek! How dare they call my mum a cow? She spends more time with them than she does with me and she's nicer to them. Plus, I'm not horrible. Okay, I am to them, but they deserve it, after all, they're totally vile and obnoxious (*cracking word*).

12.00am

Still can't sleep

Still seething. Also, v. excited about tomorrow and my very first date with the Greek God. I've never had a date on a beach before. Actually, I've never had a date anywhere before. Oh God, what shall I wear? I can't wear my skinny jeans to the beach, I'll fry! I'll have to wear my bikini – the one with the padded top – with my cut-off shorts.

I wonder what it'll be like. We're obviously not going to have sex on the beach in broad daylight (*at least I don't think we will; that would be gross*). We'll probably just get to know each other a bit better on our first date, although that could be tricky as he doesn't speak much English. It might be best if I do the talking and only ask questions that need a yes/no answer. Perhaps we won't bother talking at all. He's so gorgeous I'd be happy to spend the whole day staring into his eyes. I hope he kisses me, although I'm not totally sure which way I should tilt my head. I'll keep one eye open and see what he does first. I bet he's a fantastic kisser. Then after our first date it'll only be a matter of time before we do it. I can't wait. This is it.

DAY FOUR

10.00am

Total, total disaster. Like Romeo and Juliet, Greek God and I are being kept apart against our will...

I woke up this morning to find Trevor has organised an excursion (*a better word than 'trip' which is very primary school*).

I told him I didn't want to go. Of course, I didn't tell them it was because I'd arranged to meet the Greek God on the beach. My mother would've got straight onto the FBI or Interpol or something.

Me: Mum, please. I just want to relax on the beach.

Mum: You hate the beach.

Me: Well I've changed my mind.

Trevor: Come on, Ellie, you'll love it. Epidavros is living history, a World Heritage site.

I wasn't sure if that was meant to persuade me to go or to put me off completely. Anyway, there was no way I was going to Epileptic or whatever it's called. I decided to play my trump card.

Me: If I stay here, I can get on with my English coursework. You're always telling me to study harder.

Brilliant. Inspired. Few parents willfully stand between their kids and their education.

Mum: Well, if you put it like that.

Excellent. Should I wear my black bikini or my pink all-in-one with the halter-neck straps? I could borrow Mum's sarong to cover up my whiteness.

Trevor: Nonsense. You're *always* working, Ellie. You need a break and Epidavros is an education in itself.

Mum: Trevor's right, Ellie, come with us. It'll be fun.

No. No. NO. How could she? I couldn't believe she had betrayed me again. He's clearly been practicing his voodoo/reiki stuff on her. I was incensed. What happened to 'girl power' and 'I don't need a man to make decisions for me,' Mum? I thought blood was meant to be thicker than water, but obviously not if you're a member of the stab-you-in-the-back Foster family.

Trevor: Great, that's settled, let's go.

Trevor herded us all onto a local bus which wound along a narrow road jutting out of hillside for several hours causing the evil twins to be sick, much to their delight. I was wedged up against a window next to a woman carrying a crate with chickens in it, which stank. She kept throwing me toothless grins.

12.00pm

We have just arrived at Epidermis or whatever it's called and are waiting for Trevor to buy the tickets.

Mum is trying to pacify the love child. Blue has his fingers down his throat, trying to make himself sick again as Skye watches on. I wonder what the Greek God is doing, probably snogging the nerd's girlfriend. I'm so depressed.

2.00pm

Trevor has just dragged us around a museum to look at stones of varying sizes. He warbled on about Ancient Greece (*I should point out that I am interested in Classics, but not Trevor's version – don't want the examiner thinking I'm ignorant*), while the savages pointed at the naked statues and sniggered. Mum stayed outside, under the pretext that the love child would disturb the peace of the museum with its incessant crying. Yeah, right.

Trevor: Epidavros was a site of ancient healing founded by Astelpos, who was the son of which God, Ellie? Any guesses? Skye, please don't touch Hercules' genitalia.

Me: Canute?

Trevor: Er, no. Anyway, I've saved the best for last. Let's go and visit the (*he actually paused in a bid to build some suspense*) theatre.

I think I might have really gone and done it this time...

After we left the museum, we traipsed up a short steep slope that led out to a massive open-air auditorium. It was about the size of the Milton Keynes Bowl (*I saw Lady GaGa there with Poppy: one of her father's guilt gifts*), but with rows of stone seats. It actually looked pretty cool but I wasn't going to tell Trevor that.

Trevor: Isn't it amazing? Near perfect acoustics. Built in the 4th century BC. Unbelievable. Apparently if you stand in the centre of the stage and drop a match you can hear if from all the way up there.

He pointed to the very back row of the theatre, which looked about two miles away.

Trevor: I know. Let's try it out. Ellie, you go to the very back. I'll drop a match and if you can hear it, wave your hands to let me know.

Me: What all the way up there?

Trevor: Sure, it'll be fun.

Me: But, it's boiling hot.

Mum: Ellie!

Me: Okay.

Trevor: Now all I need is a match.

Me: Mum's got a whole box full.

So, reluctantly I hauled myself to the top of the cruddy old amphitheatre. By the time I reached the back, rivers of sweat trickled down my legs and my hair clung to my face; so uncool. Thankfully, my Greek God wasn't there to see it.

I parked myself on the very top ledge and looked back down at Trevor who was standing patiently in the middle of the stage. To one side, Mum had taken refuge from the heat and was sitting under a pine tree with love child. On the other side of the stage the savages were acting out some Greek tragedy that involved them both dying at the same time. I wish.

Seeing I was in position, Trevor waved and gave me the thumbs up which I assumed was a signal that he was about to start. I yawned and thought about the Greek God getting off with that nerd's girlfriend. Life is so unfair. By the time I got back, they would be an item.

Then I heard it. It was a tiny, but definite tap that seemed to echo around the theatre. Wow! I was almost impressed. How incredible that the sound of a match hitting the ground could fill such a vast space and be heard all the way to the back of the theatre. Robbie Williams would sound brilliant here. Trevor stuck his thumb in the air above his head. His voice floated up towards me.

Trevor: Did you hear that?

It was like he was standing right next to me; I shuddered at the thought. I was about to give him the thumbs up back when something stopped me. Instead I cupped my hand around my ear, shrugged my shoulders and shook my head to indicate that no sound had reached me.

Trevor: Okay, I'll try a coin.

I folded my arms and sat back, enjoying the sight as Trevor fished a coin out of his pocket. He held it up high and let it fall on to the metal plate in the centre of auditorium. It sounded like someone had just crashed two cymbals together. Amazing! Trevor's voice reached me again.

Trevor: How about that?

I shrugged my shoulders.

Trevor: I don't understand it. It definitely says in the guidebook that you can hear the smallest noise from the back of the theatre.

He wandered off. Thank God, I stretched out on the stone slab to soak up some rays, thinking that was the end of it. Moments later, Trevor reappeared carrying – with some difficulty – a large stone. The man's incorrigible (*not sure what it means, but Mrs Duce is always calling Jamie Harbinger incorrigible. And like Trevor, he's also a pain in the arse*).

Trevor: Okay, Ellie, let's try this.

He released the stone. It splintered into a thousand pieces, sending shards skittering across the stage. It sounded like a bomb had gone off. Several tourists nearby jumped with fright. Instinctively, I clasped my ears to shield them from the noise. Trevor looked hopefully in my direction. He stuck both thumbs into the air.

Trevor: Well? Did you hear that Ellie?

Hear it? It nearly burst my eardrums! By now, the heat was giving me a headache and even making Trevor look a right idiot was losing its thrill. I was about to wave and shout down, 'Yep, I heard that one alright' when two police officers in dark blue uniforms with guns appeared either side of Trevor.

Trevor: Ah, malaka, officers. What can I do for you?

The officers lunged at Trevor, dividing his arms and legs between him and dragging him away from the stage. Wow, if only real theatre was like that.

Trevor: What do you think you are doing? I'm English, you know.

I always thought I would relish the sight of Trevor being arrested. In fact, I've often dreamt of this moment (*although I always imagined that it would involve the Metropolitan Police and a large quantity of drugs*) but, strangely, I felt quite bad.

As the officers wrestled Trevor away, Mum leapt to her feet, clutching the love child and raced after them.

Mum: Where are you taking him? I'm his girlfriend, these are his children. We have a right to know where you are taking him.

Even the savages stopped pummelling each other and looked worried.

✰ ✰ ✰ ✰ ✰

7.20pm – **Still at Epicentre police station.**

Mum's on her mobile having a row with someone at the British Embassy in Athens.

Mum: I demand that you come down here and get my boyfriend out of jail. He's done nothing wrong. No, I don't want the number of a lawyer in Athens. No, I won't calm down. I've seen *Midnight*

Express three times, I know what these foreign jails are like. Hello? Hello?

I feel a bit sorry for her. She's borderline hysterical, although I don't know what a film about late night trains has got to do with anything. I think I'll try and put the whole episode into perspective, play it down.

Me: Mum, once they realise it's all a mistake they'll let him go.

Mum: Yes, but what state will he be in by then? I have heard about what goes on in these places. And what with his eye problem and his ponytail! Omigod, it doesn't bear thinking about.

I can tell she is about to cry so I've gone and sat next to the savages, who are unusually subdued. Even the love child seems to be munching its Cheetos more thoughtfully.

All thoughts of meeting my gorgeous Greek God have been dispelled by this crisis. Much as I loathe Trevor, I don't want to be the person responsible for sending him down for ten years for desecrating (*fabulous word. I read it in the Norbury Examiner as in 'Yobs Desecrate Statue of Baden Powell Outside Scout Hut'*) a World Heritage site. Two years would be enough.

9.30pm – Back at the hovel.

Trevor is a free man. He was released on bail (*actually he wasn't, I just wanted to demonstrate to the examiner my understanding of legal procedures*). In the end, a Greek policeman shouted at him for a bit and then let him go.

The savages actually ran up and hugged him. I never realised they were capable of that kind of affection. Mum was ecstatic, although she almost ended up in the slammer herself after calling the Greek police 'a bunch of fascists'.

Trevor was quite relaxed about it all and just referred to it as 'one of life's learning experiences'. Only an idiot could view a stretch inside with a bunch of perverts in a positive light. The man's demented.

As we left the police station, Trevor held the door open and waited for me.

Trevor: You could hear me all along, couldn't you?

My cheeks felt hot, must be sunburn.

Me: Um...Yeah.

DAY FIVE

10.00am

We got back last night and I went straight to my cell, hoping the day's events and, more importantly, my part in them would all be forgotten by today. Some hope.

12.00pm – The beach.

Mum is being a bit cool towards me, so Trevor has obviously grassed me up and is going to milk this for all it's worth. Loser. I didn't mean to get him arrested. He's clearly trying to drive a wedge between me and Mum. She is so blinded by love, she just can't see it.

The savages also seem to sense that I had a hand in getting their dad put away and are avoiding me. They have given me a wide berth all morning and have spent their time re-enacting the moment Trevor got nicked, although their version involves guns and violent injury. I even offered to let them bury me in sand again, but they just ran off screaming.

Gorgeous Greek God has also turned up but even he has completely ignored me. Perhaps news of what happened at Epi-whatsit has reached his ears. If only he knew the hell of living with Trevor, I'm sure he would understand my plight.

Right now, it's obvious: everyone hates me.

TEXT TO POPPY:

Got Trevor arrested.
No one will talk to me.

But there is no reply. Even the wonderful, sophisticated, mature Poppy doesn't want to know me.

10.30pm

My pillow (stone) is damp with tears. How could they do this to me?

I hate them. I hate them all. Mum and Trevor are GETTING MARRIED. Apparently, Trevor's spell inside prison (*God, it was only a couple of hours*) made Mum realise how much he meant to her, so she proposed to him and he accepted.

No! No! No! I can't believe I actually felt guilty when he was arrested. I wish he'd got life now.

I should've spotted the signs. Mum and Trevor took us to a pizzeria in the village. That should've been enough to set the alarm bells ringing. I'd just finished my Sloppy Giuseppe, or the Greek equivalent, when Trevor tapped his glass with a knife to get our attention.

Trevor: Order! Order! We have an announcement to make.

He sounded serious. For a minute, I thought they were going to tell me that I was being taken into care because I got Trevor banged up on false charges.

Trevor: As you all know, Elaine and I have been seeing each other for some time. When I first met Elaine, I was stunned when she agreed to go out with me (*you're not the only one, mate*). She was beautiful, not just on the outside, but on the inside as well (*are we talking about the same woman here?*)

Trevor turned to Mum and winked at her, only this time I think he meant to do it on purpose. I glanced across at Blue, who had his fingers down his throat and was pretending to throw up. I knew how he felt. I wanted to hurl too, only there was a large lump wedged in my throat stopping me. Probably cancer, from all the stress Trevor has caused me.

Trevor: Our love for each other has grown over the last couple of years and was further cemented by the arrival of our beautiful baby. The icing on the cake has been this holiday, our first together as a family.

To be honest, I was getting a bit bored by now. Even Skye was more interested in something she'd dug out of her left nostril.

Trevor: The truth is, Elaine and I were happy with the way things were, then yesterday's abhorrent miscarriage of justice (*Trevor may be an idiot, but he doesn't half know some long words; I'd have never have come up with any of those*) happened and everything changed.

I looked up. Could it be that they had realised their relationship was never going to work? That they had finally agreed to end this charade (*great word, rubbish game*) and go their separate ways? I found myself holding my breath.

Then Mum smiled at Trevor and took his hand.

Mum: Yes, it made us see just how much we mean to each other.

Trevor: Which is why we've decided to make our relationship official. We're getting married.

And there it was. Trevor had ruined my life totally with three words: we're getting married. I was too smacked in the gob to speak. I think I might put myself into care.

Skye: Who's getting married?

Mum: Your dad and I.

Blue: I hate you. I hate you! You promised you wouldn't marry her.

I looked at mum with a 'see-it's-not-just-me-whose-life-you're-ruining' expression.
    Blue pointed at Mum.

Blue: She's horrible. Ellie's horrible.

Me: Now, wait a minute.

Mum: Trevor, you didn't mention that you had told the kids you wouldn't marry me.

Trevor: Elaine, they're upset, they don't know what they're saying.

Me: Sounds clear enough to me.

Mum and Trevor: Shut up Ellie, you're not helping!

Blue leapt out of his chair and ran off, closely followed by Skye. I would have joined them but I don't break into a run unless it is serious like someone is shooting at me (and in any case Trevor went tearing after them). Love child can't walk yet, so also stayed put. But it has to be said that the kids stood united on this one: Mum and Trevor getting hitched is the worst news any of us have **ever had.**

☆ ☆ ☆ ☆ ☆

11.00pm

I'm in my cell, contemplating (*another top word, thanks to my thesaurus*) my fate, which involves being holed up in Norbury with Mum, Trevor, the savages and the love child. I could run away and live on the streets, if they weren't so dirty.

The newly-engaged couple are currently trying to persuade Blue and Skye that 'nothing's going to change' and they will 'always be loved'. Heard that one before.

I'm thinking about Dad and Delph. Would they get married now too? If they did, I could go and live with them. I suggested it to Dad once just after Mum banned me from going to the school discos for not doing my homework. He said it was a great idea and that he would like nothing more, but that it was important for a girl to be near her mother during her teenage years. But if he marries Delph perhaps that will change things. Delph is cool. She lets me borrow her make up. She'd be a great stepmother. I bet she doesn't wear sheepskin rugs on the beach.

DAY SIX

9.00am

OH NO!!...

Received emergency call from Poppy. Could only talk for a second before she had to hang up, but apparently her dad's read her texts and he's now on the hunt for the men who have been having it away with his daughter. (*In all fairness, it's probably the other way around. Poppy says her dad is in total denial that his little girl has grown up and is in touch with her sexuality. I'd like to be in touch with my sexuality – I'm nearly sixteen, after all – but I don't really know where to find it.*)

What if Poppy's dad calls my mum and tells her what I've written to Poppy???!! I'll be grounded until I am old and past it – like, 35!!

The hovel is like a morgue. Mum has told me that she is taking me and the love child to the beach to give Trevor the opportunity to spend some quality time with Blue and Skye, i.e. persuade them that his marrying Mum is a fantastic idea.

11.00am – The beach.

It may be baking hot, but things are definitely a bit cool in the Foster family. Mum and I have barely exchanged two words since we left the hovel (*but I've been keeping an eye on her phone and am ready to pounce if it so much as beeps*). It's not my fault she's marrying an idiot. I thought engagements were meant to be happy occasions.

Me: So, when are you getting hitched?

Mum: Ellie, do you have to be so awkward all the time?

Me: I only asked if you had set a date.

Mum: You know full well that we haven't.

Me: No, Mum, I don't know anything. Until last night, I thought you would realise what a dork Trevor is and ditch him as soon as we got back to Norbury.

Mum: Trevor's not a dork.

And then it came, right on cue, as it always does, the 'fifth a-mum-dment', as I call it.

Mum: You know, Ellie, if you haven't got anything nice to say, don't say anything at all.

Me: Do you think you'll wear white?

Mum: Right, that's it. Not another word.

So I haven't uttered another word and neither has she, which is actually quite good news because if Poppy's dad calls and spills the beans about our pact, hopefully Mum will have the decency to honour the fact that she isn't talking to me.

12.00pm

I've just spotted Gorgeous Greek God with the nerd and his girlfriend. The three of them are strolling along the water's edge. She is lovely. I bet she's done it. Poppy says you can always tell when someone has done it. They have a knowing look on their face and are less irritable.

12.15pm

Life is worth living again...

I was just lazing about in the water, trying not to get my hair wet when the Gorgeous Greek God, whose name is Taki by the way, just swam right up to me.

Taki: Hi.

Me: Hi.

Taki: You no come to beach yesterday.

Me: Family.

Taki: Good. Family important.

Me: Yes.

Taki: I Taki.

Me: I Ellie, I mean, I'm Ellie.

Taki: A beautiful name for a beautiful girl.

Me: Er...

Taki: Your hair is like *fotia*, fire. It is so, so red.

Me: Titian, actually.

Taki: And your skin is so, so white, like flour.

Me: Er...

Taki: I see you later, beautiful Ellie.

And he swam off. I wanted to shout after him. When? When will I see you again? But he was already headed for the shore.

My head was a jumble of emotions. He actually admired my hair and my skin. Well, I think he did. He got the colours right, anyway. He definitely said I was beautiful. No one has ever called me beautiful before. (*Jamie Harbinger had too much cider at his fifteenth birthday and said I was pretty fit, but I think he was on a dare.*)

I got out of the water. My legs were a bit wobbly. I was grateful to reach my towel without collapsing. Swimming really takes it out of you.

Mum: Was that boy bothering you?

Me: What boy?

Mum: The one you were talking to.

Me: He was nowhere near me. The angle you're sitting at must've made it look like we were close to each other. It's called an optical illusion (*good to throw in a bit of science*).

Mum: I'm going back to the villa.

Villa? Talk about deluded.

Me: Okay, I'm going to stay for a while. Give you and Trevor a bit of space. You don't need me hanging around. I'll make my own way back in a bit.

Brilliant. A stroke of genius. It just came to me in a flash. (*Miss Bartlett calls it 'thinking on your feet'. Actually I'm lying on a towel, but I think it still counts.*)

Mum: Ellie, that really is very sweet of you.

I think she genuinely meant it too.

Me: Everything'll be alright, Mum.

Not that I was really feeling that but I needed her to go away.

Mum: Thank you Ellie, I needed to hear that.

Mum packed her beach bag and picked up the love child. As she trudged down the beach I thought I heard a sniff, but I wasn't sure.

✦ ✦ ✦ ✦ ✦

5.00pm

Just had the best time of my life...

Taki came up to me just as soon as Mum left. He sat beside me on my towel, so close he was almost touching me. His skin is the colour of smooth peanut butter and his damp, tight curls looked like they had been sprinkled with diamonds. I had to keep looking away to catch my breath.

Taki told me he was a waiter. Actually, he mimed somebody

carrying a tray and I guessed. I also worked out that he finishes work at 1.00am and wants to meet me in the village square tonight; fabulous! I'll have to slip out without anyone seeing which, assuming Poppy's dad doesn't call and totally ruin everything, shouldn't be too difficult. They're all so wrapped up in themselves they probably won't even notice.

7.00pm

Hooray! Soon it'll be bye-bye Trevor...

When I returned, Mr and Mrs Gnome were sitting outside on the steps of their ruin. They smiled and said something incomprehensible (*another great word, thanks to Mrs Duce: 'Ellie, your writing is quite frankly incomprehensible'*). I smiled back, but didn't dare say anything. Then just as I was about to go inside and join the rest of the zoo, I heard someone call my name. I turned around to see GM coming towards me, dressed in a white trouser suit and a floppy sun hat. Behind her, laden with bags, was a big, burly Greek man in a white shirt, unbuttoned to his navel.

GM: Ellie, darling, how wonderful to see you!

We hugged each other although I was distracted by the man's chest-hair poking out of his shirt, which was long enough to plait.

Me: GM, I'm so glad you're here. It's been awful.

I gulped back the tears.

GM: Don't worry darling, you can tell me all about it later. Oh, by the way, this is my latest beau, Stratos. We met on the ferry on the way over. I took one look at him and thought 'you can enter my sphere anytime'. Get it? Strat-o-sphere?

Me: GM, you can't say that to me. I'm your granddaughter. Er, hello Stratos.

Stratos: Me strong. Like bull.

As opposed to Trevor who is weak. Like stick insect.

GM: Now, don't tell me you haven't picked up some nice young Greek man? On second thoughts, with Attila-the-Mum keeping guard, probably not.

At that point, Mum and Trevor appeared in the doorway of the hovel. They didn't seem quite so pleased to see GM as I was.
GM turned to me and raised her eyebrows.

GM: Oh God, I'd forgotten about him.

Trevor had an 'oh no, not her' look on his face. Mum stepped forwards and hugged GM quickly.

Mum: GM, lovely to see you. We were hoping you'd make it.

Two lies in one sentence. Impressive.

Trevor: Hello GM. Who's your friend?

GM: This is Stratos.

Trevor: Hello Stratos.

Stratos: Me strong. Like bull.

GM: He doesn't speak much English, but who cares? I'm not interested in his conversational skills.

Mum: GM! Not in front of Ellie. She's at an impressionable age.

GM: Good, hopefully she'll be as impressed by Stratos as I am.

Trevor: Er, are you planning to stay for, er, a while?

GM: Don't panic Trevor, we're going to check into the hotel in the village. We just dropped by to say hello. So, aren't you going to invite us in for a drink?

We all piled into the kitchen. Mum sidled up to me.

Mum: You haven't told her about me and Trevor, have you?

Me: No, why? Is it a secret?

Mum: No, it's just that we need to choose the right moment.

Too right you do. GM is going to go ballistic when she finds out about you and Trevor.

Inside the hovel, GM produced a bottle of Ouzo and insisted we all had some, even the savages had a little sip. They perked up no end and kept shouting for 'more liquorice'. Then Stratos got up and left quite suddenly to go somewhere but as he doesn't speak English no one could work out where he had gone. He just kept showing us his biceps so it must have involved heavy lifting of some kind. As soon as he was out of sight, Mum turned on GM.

Mum: How old is he, GM? He looks about my age.

GM: He's rather divine, isn't he? Solid muscle, not an ounce of fat on him. Actually, he's a year younger than you.

Mum: GM, you really shouldn't behave like this.

GM: Really, tell me, how I should behave? Like you?

I think the expression, Mum, is touché. Go GM!

Mum: Trevor and I love each other.

GM: Darling, you sound like a couple of lovesick teenagers.

That is an insult to teenagers. If I had a boyfriend (which hopefully by tonight I will) we certainly wouldn't behave like Mum and Trevor. You'd never get me in cheesecloth for a start and I wouldn't be seen dead with someone who wears socks with sandals.

Mum and Trevor arranged to meet GM later for a family meal. It's going to be a long night. If it weren't for the fact I'm meeting Taki later, I don't think I could cope.

☆ ☆ ☆ ☆ ☆

11.05pm

Can no one see how wrong it is for Mum to marry Trevor? Am I the only sane voice in a wilderness of insanity? (Does that qualify as poetry?)...

Trevor found us a small, 'typically Greek' taverna in the village. It was so small in fact that it only had two tables in its front courtyard. We pushed them together so we could all fit around them. Stratos still hadn't returned.

The waiter didn't seem to like us much as he kept scowling and muttering to the woman, presumably his wife, in a low whisper. There weren't even any menus. We sat for a bit, wondering what to do, until suddenly a load of food arrived. It looked delicious but I couldn't eat a thing; I was so nervous about meeting Taki. Half way through the meal, Mum stopped and turned to GM.

Mum: We've something to tell you.

Fantastic, I thought, here come the fireworks. Once GM knew Mum and Trevor were getting married she'd put a stop to it. I wasn't sure what she would do – threats to boycott their big day could seriously backfire; Mum and Trevor would probably view a no-show by GM as a wedding gift – but I was sure she would come up with something.

GM held up her hands to interrupt Mum.

GM: Don't tell me. You and Trevor are getting married.

Mum glared at me.

Mum: How do you know?

GM: Mother's intuition. Well, what can I say?

I held my breath. I knew GM would give them both a piece of her mind. She would probably go on about how selfish Mum was and how she had completely ignored the psychological damage her marrying a hippy would do to me. Mum would burst into tears, but would see sense and call off this ridiculous farce of a marriage. Years from now she would thank GM for her near miss.

GM: Congratulations! I hope you'll be very happy together.

How could this be? How could she? Had Trevor bewitched her as well with his reiki-hocus-pocus nonsense? It seems that GM, like my mother, has totally betrayed me. Can no one see that Trevor is

111

a total plonker? Am I the only one? Sometimes being right is a lonely place to be. I'm drowning, not waving (*okay, I stole that from a poem we did in Year 9. I'm not sure it fits here, but it sounds good*).

We finished our meal. Mum and Trevor kept catching each other's eye and smirking at each other. Every now and then Trevor would squeeze Mum's knee and she would giggle. She even fed him some of her squid - how disgusting.

GM spent the whole meal going on about how gorgeous Stratos is until she started on about how good he was in bed and Trevor asked her to stop.

At the end of the meal, Trevor threw a 50 euro note on the table, shouting 'malaka' at the owners, who had spent the whole meal sitting in the corner of the courtyard just staring at us. No wonder no one else was there.

Trevor: Great food, but miserable service. The Greek economy depends on the tourist industry. They need people like us.

GM: But not when you are so rude to them.

Trevor: What do you mean?

GM: He served you a banquet and you called him a tosser.

Trevor: No, I didn't.

GM: Yes, you did. Malaka is Greek for tosser. Everyone knows that.

Trevor covered his face with his hands.

Trevor: Omigod, I don't believe it!

Mum started to laugh, followed by GM and even Trevor. Soon all three were falling about holding their sides. Personally, I don't find insulting people in their own language that funny. In fact, it's almost certainly Greek-ist. The three of them laughed and joked as we left the restaurant while the rest of us trailed behind miserably.

As we arrived back at the hovel, GM dropped back to speak to me.

GM: You're not happy, are you, Ellie?

I must have swallowed a midge or something, because all of sudden I was finding it hard to speak. GM waited until I was ready.

Me: No, I'm not. I don't understand what she sees in him, GM.

GM: Well I can't say I really see it either. I certainly don't like the way he winks at me all the time. I wouldn't have thought I was his type.

Me: I drank one of his contact lenses.

GM squeezed my arm and laughed:

GM: Brilliant!

Me: How come if you don't like Trevor, you're so pleased they're getting married?

GM: Look Ellie, he might not be my choice – all that long hair, really not my thing – and he's not your choice, but he is your mother's choice and he does make her happy.

Me: Dad made her happy.

GM: No, your dad used to make her laugh sometimes. He didn't make her happy. There's a difference. Then the laughing stopped and they found there was nothing left. Stratos darling, you're back!

Stratos appeared outside Mr and Mrs Gnome's shack. He

beckoned to us to join him. So we followed him around the ruin into the Gnomes' back garden where Mr Gnome was cooking fish on a barbecue and knocking back the Ouzo with Mrs Gnome and Stratos. Mr Gnome poured some Ouzo into some spare glasses and passed them around.

Then Mrs Gnome got up, took me by the hand into the hovel which wasn't a hovel at all inside. In fact, it was quite palatial (*I got that from Mum's* Hello! *mags; apparently Jordan's gaff is 'palatial' – it just looked very white to me*) with a fully-fitted kitchen, including a dishwasher and a hob.

Mrs Gnome then led me into a darkened room with a huge plasma TV flickering in the corner (*we don't have one of those in Norbury*). On a brown leather sofa in front of it were two figures engrossed in *Spiderman*.

Mrs Gnome turned the light on and said something to the couple in Greek. They turned around and looked up at me. My mouth fell open. It was the geek from the beach and his beautiful girlfriend. They smiled at me.

Geek: Hi, d'you want to join my sister and I? My grandmother thinks you'll be bored with the others.

Well, she got that right. Sister? Well, that explains it.

Nerd's sister: We're watching *Spiderman*. Sorry, it's the best we could do; this place isn't exactly up on the latest films. I'm Sophia. This is my brother George. Come and sit down.

How could someone as gorgeous and sophisticated-looking as Sophia watch such childish films as *Spiderman*?

Me: Okay, thanks. I'm Ellie.

The two of them parted to make room for me. I dropped down on the sofa between them.

Sophia: Do you like Greece, Ellie?

Me: Yes, it's lovely. Your English is excellent.

Sophia: Thank you, I want to be an English teacher when I leave school.

Me: Really? (*Oh God, not another bloody teacher*)

George dragged his eyes away from the television screen and looked at me. His face was solemn. I wondered what was coming next.

George: You know, Ellie, you should be careful with Taki.

Of all the cheek! How dare he? Just because he's a boring geek, it doesn't give him the right to tell me how to live my life.

Sophia: George is right. Taki is a *kamaki*.

Me: So? I don't see anything wrong in someone taking interest in the martial arts.

She clearly just wants Taki for herself. George burst out laughing.

George: *Kamaki* is a Greek word, it means harpoon. We use it to describe boys who chase women.

Me: Right.

An awkward silence closed around us and we turned to look at the screen where Spiderman had just caught a baddie in his web.
    It was a relief to receive a text from Poppy.

TEXT FROM POPPY:

Things are bad. Dad asking
really awkward questions.

TEXT TO POPPY:

Nightmare. Meeting Taki
in four hours. Wish me
luck.

TEXT FROM POPPY:

Go girl. Hide your
phone from oldies.

Oh God, this is all I need. If Poppy's dad calls Mum, I am so dead.
Perhaps I should accidentally drop her phone in a rock pool or
something, just to make sure.

Trevor arrived with a plate of kebabs.

Trevor: Hey dudes. What's going down?

Dudes? Where does he think he is? The Bronx?

Trevor: You guys getting to know each other? You'll be swapping
CDs before you know it. Quite like a bit of Zeppelin myself.

George: Me too.

There's a surprise. This was rapidly turning into a geek-fest. And
nobody buys CDs anymore.

Sophia: And me.

No, it can't be possible. I dragged myself to my feet and went back outside. GM was sitting on Stratos' lap curling his chest hair around her forefinger and giggling. Mum looked excruciatingly embarrassed (*now she knows how I feel 95 per cent of the time*). The savages were howling at the full moon and the love child was fast asleep. I ambled over to the savages.

Me: Good howling.

Blue: Go away.

Me: Charming.

Skye: We don't like you. You're mean.

Me: I don't like you either.

Skye: We don't want your mum to marry Trevor.

Me: Well, that makes three of us.

Then it dawned on me: all this time we had been working against each other but we all agreed on one thing: Mum and Trevor couldn't get married at any cost. Perhaps, if we joined forces and worked together, we could split them up once and for all.

Me: You know I might be able to come up with a plan to stop them getting married, but I need your help.

The evil twins hesitated and then produced grins that bordered on psychotic.

Blue: How? An accident?

Me: That might be taking it too far. Leave it with me. I'll come up with something.

And so the cave children and I have struck a truce; we would split Mum and Trevor up for good. Things are looking up. In a couple of hours, I will be in Taki's arms and by the end of the holiday Trevor will be history.

We left the party soon afterwards, as GM and Stratos were getting a bit frisky and Mum said she wasn't prepared to sit back and watch her daughter being corrupted by 'someone who should know better'. What a hypocrite!

1.00am

Just half an hour to go before d-day. (That's deflowering day. Poppy's expression, not mine. I've no idea what flowers have got to do with sex.) I'm just waiting for everyone to go to bed.

3.30am

I am totally in love...

Geeky George is totally wrong. Taki was charming, the perfect gentleman. Okay, I didn't actually 'do it', but that's cool, he's obviously prepared to wait.

When I was sure everyone was asleep, I climbed out of my cell window. The night had cooled right down and the air was really still. I looked up and the sight took by breath away. The night sky looked like a giant hand had sprinkled a pot of glitter over it; I'd never seen the sky like that before. You don't get stars like that in

Norbury (*not unless you count Marsha Blunt who had a bit part in Hollyoaks ten years ago and now runs a nail bar in the High Street. Ha ha!*).

If I hadn't been meeting Taki, I could've sat outside the hovel all night just looking at the stars. I guess love makes you notice things like that.

I made my way through the dark streets, passing the restaurant where we had eaten with GM. It was closed. It's never going to make money like that. I know about failed businesses; after all, I do live Norbury.

I reached the village square where there were loads of people milling around. Perhaps they really are vampires. Guess this place isn't as dead as I first thought...I sat on the wall next to the kiosk and waited. Minutes later Taki appeared and the feeling that he may have been watching me before making his entrance quickly passed.

Taki: Beautiful Ellie.

I can't get used to that. Perhaps he's being ironic.

Me: Hi.

Taki: Want to have fun?

Me: Sure.

Actually, if I'm honest, I wasn't sure at all. What did he mean by fun? Should I have mentioned the fact that I hadn't even done tongues? I tried it with Martin Hopegood when we were in Year 9 but his tongue felt like a big fat slug had crawled into my mouth, collapsed and died, so I bit it. He called me frigid and stormed off (*that will definitely have to come out, don't want the examiner or anyone thinking I'm a crap kisser*). I told Poppy who instantly appointed herself my 'special needs' kissing teacher. We had a few tries with a pillow, but I nearly suffocated myself. In the end, Poppy just said 'put your head to one side and let them do all the work'. That's easy for her to say – boys want to kiss her.

Taki: Great. *Ela*, Ellie! Come.

He took me by the hand and showed me his moped.

Taki: You like?

Me: Yes.

When will men realize that women are just not into gadgets in the same way? Taki climbed on and nodded to the back seat. I didn't know what to do. If I refused to get on he would dump me. If I got on the back, he could take me anywhere. He could be a mad axe-man, for all I knew. Plus, I'd forgotten to get some more hairspray. A small part of me hoped Mum would appear and shout at me to go home. She didn't. Too busy being all loved up with Trevor.

Me: Where are we going?

Taki: Not far. You see. I good boy.

I hesitated.

Me: Okay. *(Well, I didn't want anyone else thinking I was frigid.)*

Taki started the bike. I climbed on and we roared away. I looked across at the restaurant and saw George and Sophia having a drink. Their grandparents must be much more relaxed than my mother. Or perhaps they don't have any rapists here. Anyway I thought it was good to have witnesses. The only problem was that they didn't look up. Taki swung the bike through the narrow streets. We even passed the hovel and then we were out into the dark, dense countryside, away from the village. Every now and then, he turned around and laughed.

Taki: Eeets fun, no?

Me: Yes. (*No, stop, I want to get off.*)

To my relief, the bike pulled up alongside the bay where we had spent most of our days. It looked different in the moonlight.

Taki stopped the bike. We got off and he took my hand and led me onto the sand. As my eyes adjusted to the scene, I was comforted by the fact that we were not alone on the beach. In the distance, dark figures sat all along the seashore. There was even a couple frolicking (*great word*) in the sea. The sight of company close at hand soothed my worries. I relaxed and sat down next to Taki. He lay down and pulled me down next to him, holding me in his arms. We both stared up at the sky.

Taki: Eets beautiful no?

Me: Yes, beautiful.

Taki told me the Greek names for some of the constellations, which I can't remember now (*which is shame as it could've been worth a few extra marks*), but they sounded much better in Greek.

Taki: You see that star there?

Me: The bright one?

Taki: Yes, bright and beautiful. That's Ellie's star.

Me: Really?

Taki: Really.

Suddenly Taki leant over me and kissed me on the lips. He smelt musky and his breath was a bit garlicky. I didn't say anything as I didn't want to spoil the moment. There was plenty of time to introduce him to Colgate.

He kissed me again. I followed Poppy's advice and let him do all the work. It felt wonderful, warm and soft. His kisses flowed right through me. They were much better than Martin Hopegood's 'clamping' method and I realised then that Martin was as inexperienced as I was.

Taki's kisses grew harder and more urgent (*I got that from one of Mum's Sidney Sheldon novels*). His lips pushed mine apart and his tongue slid into my mouth. We were snogging, actually snogging and his tongue didn't feel even remotely slug-like. His face was rough and unshaven against mine, but minor abrasions were a small price to pay for this lovely tingling feeling that had started in mouth and was now spreading through my veins.

Taki put his hand under my T-shirt. I flinched with the shock of his cold hand on my warm skin. I wondered where it was heading and was contemplating trying to remove it without him noticing when I was distracted by a noise.

Stratos: Me strong. Like bull.

GM: Stratos! Stratos! Put me down. You beast!

I sat up abruptly to see two dark figures emerge from the water, one carrying the other.

Me: Omigod.

Taki held out his hands in surprise.

Taki: What, you no like?

Me: No – I mean yes. But my grandmother is here.

Taki: Grandmother? Where? You are sure?

But the threat was enough to make him sit bolt upright. Clearly, grannies are a force to be reckoned with in Greece.

Me: Shsssh, no talk.

Stratos set GM down on the beach. She slapped him playfully and then the two of them starting to make their way up the beach towards us. It was then that I realised a pile of clothes sitting just feet away from my head belonged to them. This was turning into a disaster of massive proportions. GM had already betrayed me once tonight. If she realised it was me, I was sure she would blab to my mother who would launch a public inquiry into my behaviour. I couldn't let her know I was here on the beach with a Greek boy who was at least two years older than me.

I grabbed Taki by his T-shirt.

Me: Kiss me.

Taki: Okay.

I desperately hoped Stratos and GM would ignore this couple making out on the beach. Surely it's impolite to stare at people when they are kissing? I never look at Trevor and Mum when they are at it, mainly because it makes me want to hurl.

Then another thought suddenly filled me with horror. I'm not a religious person, but I found myself praying that GM and Stratos wouldn't get carried away and end up 'doing it' on the beach right next to us. Urgh! The idea! I just couldn't bear that. I would just have to break cover and make a run for it.

I pulled myself together. What was I thinking? There was no way GM would be able to tell it was me. It was far too dark and I was lying on top of Taki, my face completely obscured. I could relax, I was totally safe.

GM: Hello Ellie.

Me: Er, hi Gran, er, GM.

How embarrassing. I pushed myself off Taki and sat up. GM's hair was still dripping with seawater, but at least they'd had the decency to keep their underwear on when they went swimming. They towelled themselves dry and got dressed.

GM: Don't worry, darling, your secret is safe with me.

When they had finished, Stratos knelt down beside Taki and whispered into his ear. Taki nodded solemnly. Then the two of them sauntered off down the beach, hand in hand.
I turned to Taki.

Me: What did he say to you?

Taki: Nothing. We go now. Eet's late.

Taki drove me back to the village and dropped me off at the top of the road leading to the hovel. I clambered off the bike and stood close to him, enjoying the warmth from his body in the cool night air. He picked some stray hairs from my face and stroked my cheek.

Taki: Ellie, you are beautiful. I love you.

I gasped as he pulled me tight to him and gave me a long hard kiss – no tongues this time. When he put me down I was still struggling to breathe. He laughed.

Taki: I see you again.

Me: Yes, please. (*I can't believe I said please! How desperate must that have sounded? Poppy would be well angry if I told her.*)

Taki: Okay, tomorrow night.

I drifted back to the hovel, climbed back through the window and lay down in my bed. But I couldn't sleep.

TEXT TO POPPY:

In love. Great snogger.
Second base is awesome!
Can't wait for third.

Okay so a slight exaggeration but I would definitely catch up tomorrow.

TEXT FROM POPPY:

Great stuff. Make the most of it.
Oldies are on to us. Dad threatening to
call police if I don't 'fess up and I'm
not allowed out.

Oh God, that sounds serious. But if Poppy's dad is tied up with getting witness statements from the hotel staff and acting as Poppy's jailer, then hopefully he'll forget to call Mum. I crossed everything I could think of.

DAY SEVEN

11.00am – **On the beach**.

I'm still on cloud nine hundred and ninety-nine. Even our 'family trip' to the beach can't dampen the way I feel. Is it love? It could be. I don't know what love feels like, but I know I have never felt like this before. I really am flying without wings.

GM and Stratos have joined us. GM keeps winking at me and is so indiscreet about last night that I'm sure it is only a matter of time before Mum realises that something's up. Stratos in is the sea hurling Blue and Skye into the water.

No sign of Taki, but George and Sophia are here. She's nice, but he's a total loser and they obviously don't know Taki that well. Omigod, perhaps George is JEALOUS. What a fantastic thought. I've never had two boys fighting over me before. Poppy says there's no feeling like it. Guys are always scrapping over her.

12.00pm

I've decided to go for a dip, mainly to escape GM's innuendos.

12.40pm

Was having a nice swim, until Blue appeared alongside me.

Blue: Skye and I have got a plan.

Me: Really? That's nice. A plan for what, precisely?

Blue: To split Elaine and Dad up.

Oh God! In my loved-up state, I'd totally forgotten our plans to put an end to the nonsense that is Trevor and Mum's relationship.

Me: Okay, what have you got?

Blue: We push Elaine off a cliff.

Me: Hold on. Why my mum? Why not Trevor?

Blue: He's got more kids.

Me: We're not pushing anyone off any cliffs, understood?

Blue: Poison?

Me: No!

Blue: Electrocution?

Me: No.

Blue: What then?

Me: I don't know, I'll come up with something.

Blue: You promised.

Me: And Ellie Foster never breaks her promises (*lie*).

I winked at him conspiratorially (*check spelling*). In truth, my head was still spinning from the events of last night. I really hadn't had time to think about how to split up the lovebirds although I was fairly sure that death was not an option.

1.40pm

I'm totally bored and there's still no sign of Taki. This is turning into the longest day ever. Trevor has his head buried in a book, *Buddhism without Beliefs* and is no doubt conjuring up more ways to keep my mum under his spell.

Mum has finally reached chapter two of *A Suitable Boy*. GM and Stratos are draped all over each other. She keeps going on about the Foster family's preference for Greek men. She's so obvious. Blue and Skye keep staring at me, with an air of expectancy.

1.50pm

I think Blue has just tried to murder my mother, although part of me wishes I'd just let him get on with it.

Blue: Elaine, do you want to go for a walk on the rocks?

Mum: Thanks Blue, that would be lovely.

Me: No, don't.

Mum: Why not?

Me: Because I was about to ask if you wanted to go for a swim with me.

Mum: Lovely. You don't mind, do you Blue? Ellie and I spend so little time together.

I hope she realises one day that I probably just saved her life. The swim descended into the usual row over her relationship with Trevor.

Mum: This is nice. Seems a long time since we did the mother and daughter things.

Me: Mmm.

Mum: Are you enjoying your holiday?

Me: Yes (*well, bits of it*).

Mum: Ellie, I know it's difficult for you, not having anyone here the same age as you.

Me: It's okay. (*I've got the most gorgeous Greek boyfriend.*)

Mum: Trevor spoke to Sophia and George and they would be happy for you to go out with them one evening. They're fifteen too. In fact, George's birthday is a week after yours.

Oh God, what is it with parents (*and parent's boyfriends*) that they try and pick your friends for you? I felt myself boil inside.

Me: I'm fine on my own Mum. Please stop interfering.

Mum: Trevor just thought it would be nice for you to spend time with children your own age. He is a teacher after all, he understands teenagers far better than I do.

Me: I don't care what Trevor thinks. He just wants me out of the way so he can play happy families with you and the love child.

Mum: That's not true. He goes out of his way to spend time with you.

Me: Well, I don't want to spend time with him. And, by the way, did you know you've got a pink rash on your chest?

Mum: I think I might be allergic to wool.

And I'm allergic to Trevor.

The water was making my eyes sting so I swam away as fast as I could, leaving Mum on her own. By the time I got out of the water, Mum was already on the beach, digging holes in the sand with Blue and Skye.

GM: Surprised you have the energy to swim, Ellie.

Trevor: Right, Ellie, I've got one for you. What's a cumulus?

GM: Sounds rude.

Trevor: Give you a clue, there's none in the sky today.

Me: A type of helicopter?

Trevor: Not quite.

I couldn't stand it any longer. I'm sick of him. I want things to go back to the way they were: me and Mum curled up on the settee, watching *Eastenders*, eating a chicken tikka masala ready meal from Asda. I want rid of him once and for all.

Me: I'm going for a walk.

I headed for some rocks and found a place to sit. I gazed out to sea, hoping to come across as enig-, egnig-, *mysterious*. I was starting to get bored when I heard a voice.

George: Hello.

It took me a moment to realize that the person who had just said hello was talking to me. I looked up and geeky George was standing over me, looking like a skeleton that's been allowed maybe one meal.

Me: Oh, hi.

George: Your dad said you wanted to come out with us.

Me: Well, he was wrong. And he's not my dad.

George: Okay. What's up with his eye?

Me: He's got a twitch.

George: Right.

I looked out to sea, hoping that he would take the hint and buzz off, but he stood for a little longer and then sat down beside me on the rocks. Neither of us said anything for ages, but I could feel his eyes on me. In the end I had to say something.

Me: What? What are you looking at?

George: Why are you so sad?

Me: I'm not.

George: You are. Even when you smile, you're sad.

Me: Family stuff.

George: Ah, I know about family stuff.

I'm embarrassed to admit it, but I actually snorted. I didn't mean to, it just came out. Thank God it happened here and not at school; I'd never hear the end of it.

Me: Really?

George: My mother is married three times. I have moved house ten times and lived in four different countries. My dad lives in Switzerland, I don't see him much. That's why we spend so much time with my grandparents. Sophia and I are, how you say, 'in the path'?

Me: I think you mean 'in the way'. You're in the way.

George: Life's a beach.

Me: Yes, life's a beach.

Suddenly he stood up.

George: See you later, Ellie.

And with that, he was gone, leaving me feeling strangely empty and alone. Not that I wanted a geek like George to hang around me. I was glad he was gone. He probably made up that stuff about his family; loser.

No sooner had George ambled off when Blue and Skye's heads popped up from behind a rock.

Me: Oh God, what do you two want?

Blue: You promised to help us split up Dad and Elaine. Remember.

I looked at the two of them with their matted red hair and expectant faces. The three of us had put up with the 'Trevor and

Elaine Show' for too long; it was time to take control over our own destinies. A plan began to form in my mind. A plan that would mean my life would no longer be a 'beach'.

Me: You're right, I did promise.

Blue: So, do you have a plan?

Me: You bet I do.

Blue and Skye sat down next to me.

Blue: Do we get to use guns?

Me: Er, no. We have to be a bit more subtle than that.

Blue and Skye looked at me with blank faces. I guess eight-year-olds don't do subtle.

Me: What I mean is we have to split them up in such a way that neither of them suspects we had anything to do with it. Otherwise it won't work.

Blue and Skye nodded.

Blue: Do you mean we should kill both of them?

Me: No, it's much better than that. We're going to turn Trevor and Mum against each other. By the time we've finished, they'll hate the sight of each other.

Skye clapped her hands.

Skye: I like it, I like it.

Blue: How do we do that?

Me: Well, Trevor loves you more than anything right? So if anything was to happen to you two while Mum was meant to be looking after you, what do you think Trevor would do?

Skye: He'd send her to the naughty step – forever.

Blue: He'd be very angry.

Me: Exactly. So here's what we'll do. Tomorrow, you, Skye, me and Mum will all go swimming together. Then, I'll distract Mum while you two disappear under the water.

Blue: You mean we have to drown?

Me: Only pretend, really you've just swum to a rock and hidden behind it.

I could tell they were impressed.

Me: Then Trevor will totally blame Mum for losing you, especially as she was meant to be taking care of you. There'll be a bit of panic while he tries to find you, then you can just reappear. Tell him, you called for help, but Mum was too busy with me, that kind of thing. Do you think you can do that? (*God, I'm good. And to think that on my last report, Miss B actually said I 'lacked creativity'.*)

Blue: Sure. How about if we cut ourselves as well and pretend we were attacked by sharks?

Me: Er no, I think we'll leave it as it is, best not to complicate things.

Blue shrugged. I watched the two of them clamber back over the rocks and return to the others. Tomorrow, when it was all over, and Mum and Trevor were at each other's throats, we would go our separate ways for good.

My mind drifted back to thoughts of Taki. Would he definitely turn up tonight? Would we do 'it'? The idea made me feel nervous inside. I wonder if second base is the same in Greece as it is in England. Poppy says second base is strictly 'upstairs' (*not in the house sense*). Last night was fantastic. I think I'm ready.

11.30pm

Still waiting for everyone to go to bed.

Trevor is teaching the savages to play bridge. Mum went to the toilet about twenty minutes ago and hasn't returned. No guesses what she's doing in there. GM and Stratos have gone to a nightclub. They invited me, but Mum said no.

TEXT TO POPPY:

This is it. Will tell all
tomorrow.

1.00am

The place is totally silent now.

Everyone's in bed. I'm going right now. Tomorrow I will be a woman. Maybe even Trevor will get on my nerves less.

� ✩ ✩ ✩ ✩

2.30am

Bloody, bloody, bloody hell! I hate, hate, HATE Trevor. Forever.

DAY EIGHT

7.00am

TEXT FROM POPPY:

Well?

TEXT TO POPPY:

Trevor ruined everything.

That says it all really. Last night was a total disaster, thanks to that moron.

I climbed out of the window to go and meet Taki, but as I was leaving I ran into Trevor who was sitting outside the hovel. He said he was stargazing, but I don't believe him; Mum had clearly posted him on guard. Had Poppy's dad finally called?

I tried to be really casual and just told him that I couldn't sleep so I was going for a little walk. And then, of all the cheek, he invited himself along with me.

So the two of us traipsed around the village for about an hour, while Trevor rattled on about tectonic plates and the Richter Scale. We even passed the square where I was meant to meet Taki. There was no sign of him, of course. I could kiss goodbye to ever having a proper boyfriend with Trevor chaperoning me everywhere. He's worse than Mum. Then, of all things, he decided to get PERSONAL.

Trevor: You don't like me much, do you, Ellie?

Of course I bloody don't (*may have to remove swearing – it could cost me vital marks*). You seduce my mother (*what a repulsive thought*) and you stop me reaching second base with Antonio Banderas' better looking younger brother.

Me: Dunno (*lie*).

Trevor: Ellie, I love Elaine (*oh God, no, please, don't tell me how you FEEL about Mum. I was squirming inside*), I love everything about her (*not the fags, I'll bet*) and that includes her daughter: you.

Yes, I know who Mum's daughter is. Idiot.

Me: Right.

Trevor: I feel the same way about you as I do about my own children.

Don't even think about making me eat rabbit food.

Trevor: I want you to be happy.

Well, leave Mum alone then.

Me: Right.

Trevor: Great, glad that's settled. Look it's getting late, let's get back to the villa. See that constellation there? That's Gemini, the twins. Blue and Skye think it is named after them.

I looked up and bit my lip. I couldn't see Ellie's star any more.
    When I woke up this morning, I overheard Trevor telling Mum that he had had a 'real breakthrough' with me. Yeah, right.
GM and Stratos also left first thing this morning to go island hopping. Before she went, GM took me to one side.

GM: Ellie, it's time for us all to move on with our lives.

No idea what she meant by that. Perhaps she and Stratos are planning to get hitched. God, they're all at it!

10.00am – On the beach.

Blue has just sidled up to me.

Blue: Well? When are we going to do it?

Me: Be patient, it's all in hand.

At least last night focused my mind on how to get shot of Trevor once and for all.

Blue: I'll tell Skye.

Me: Good.

11.00am

The love between Taki and me burns as bright as ever...

Just as I was coming back with a load of choc ices, I heard someone go 'psst'. I swung round to see Taki in his waiter's uniform.

Taki: Beautiful Ellie. Where are you last night? Why you with your father?

Me: He's not my father.

Taki: Never mind. Tonight? You and me?

He rubbed his two forefingers vigorously together which confused me a bit.

Me: Okay.

I don't believe it! He is still interested in me – he must really like me.

Taki: I wait in square for beautiful Ellie.

This 'beautiful Ellie' thing was starting to get on my nerves, although I didn't say anything. I might ask him to ration saying it a bit when we're going steady.

I practically skipped back to the others, grinning like the Cheshire Cat. I would've completely forgotten about 'Operation GET RID' if Blue and Skye hadn't been glaring at me.

☆ ☆ ☆ ☆ ☆

2.00pm

Oh God, I can hardly bear to write this...

When I got back to the others, I passed the ice-creams around.

Me: Here you go, Trevor, I got you a choc ice.

Trevor: Packed full of additives, but I appreciate the thought, Ellie, thanks.

He winked at Mum, looking super-pleased with himself at the progress he had made with his girlfriend's daughter.

Mum: That eye is still really giving some gip, isn't it?

Me: Tell you what, Mum. Why don't we leave Trevor to read *Conversations with God* in peace? (*Conversations with God? I wonder if He's as bored as I am with Trevor's inane questions about dried-up river beds!*) We could take Skye and Blue over to that jetty.

Blue and Skye jumped up and down.

Blue/Skye: Yes, let's, let's, jetty, jetty!

Mum: Okay.

Trevor gave her a 'see, I told you I would get through to her' look and we headed off to the pier on the far side of the bay, leaving Trevor in charge of the love child.

On the way, we stopped to marvel at a dead jellyfish which Blue carried to the jetty on a stick. When we got there Mum made herself comfortable and watched while the three of us took in turns to jump into the deep waters below.

I pulled myself out of the water and sat on the wooden jetty next to Mum.

Mum: It's good to see you enjoying yourself, Ellie. Blue and Skye are really rather sweet, in an untamed kind of way.

Me: I'm going to go and have a look at the rock pools over there.

Mum: Fine, I'll stay here and keep an eye on these two.

I clambered over some rocks. Thank God, no one from school could see. I only do pavements. When I was about twenty metres away, I stopped and pretended to be interested in some seaweed (as if). Blue and Skye continued launching themselves off the jetty and dragging themselves out of the water only to repeat the process all over again. I hesitated for a moment. Was this really the right thing to do? It was what Blue and Skye wanted. More importantly, it's the best thing for Mum. I braced myself and then let out a scream, timing it just as Blue and Skye threw themselves off the end of the pier.

Me: Mum, come quick. I think I've stepped on a stonefish (*good to throw in a little understanding of the local marine life*).

Mum hesitated, switching back and forth like a Wimbledon spectator, from me to spot where Blue and Skye had gone into the water. I screamed again; that clinched it. She got up and ran over to me.

Me: Ow, it really hurts. Stonefish are poisonous.

Mum: Okay, darling, don't move. I'll just get Blue and Skye out of the water.

But, as planned, they had completely disappeared from sight. Only I knew that they'd swum to a boat moored nearby and were hiding behind the hull. Mum searched the waters, running up and down the jetty. I watched as she began to grow increasingly frantic.

Mum: Children, where are you? Don't play games now!

But I could tell that she didn't think this was a joke. Okay, I did feel a tiny tinge of guilt seeing my mum in so much distress, but it was for her own good. Then suddenly she held her nose and dived into the clear waters. Mum doesn't disturb her hair for anything, unless it's serious. She came back up spluttering and coughing.

Mum: Omigod, Ellie, where are they?

I looked across at the boat and saw two faces peeping around the side, grinning back at me.

Me: Dunno.

Mum: I'll have to get Trevor. Omigod, what am I going to tell him? Ellie, keep looking. Please find them!

Me: Ok!

I watched her run. I've never seen her run before; she's quite fast. She reached Trevor. Moments later he threw his book down and the two of them raced back in my direction. Other people on the beach began to take an interest in what was happening, but they seemed a little confused at the sight of a man in cut-off jeans running along the beach shouting Blue! Skye! A few of them looked upwards and agreed the sky was in fact blue, which wasn't terribly helpful.

Blue and Skye appeared from behind the boat again. I motioned to them to swim further along the coast. They gave me the thumbs up and disappeared like a couple of water babies.
Trevor and Mum arrived at the jetty, panting like dogs (*I think I've got the hang of this metaphor thing*). They were both white with terror.

Trevor: Ellie, can you see them at all?

Me: No, sorry.

Trevor stared at the calm seas, and then looked around wildly, his eyes full of panic.

Trevor: Please somebody help us! My kids are in the water, but I can't find them.

His voice sounded like it was about to crack. Mum started to sob uncontrollably. Even I started to cry and I knew where the evil twins were.

Trevor took a deep breath and leapt into the water. By now people had begun to emerge from the nearby restaurants attracted by the shouting and crying. Several waiters dropped their trays and leapt into the water as well, while others stood on the jetty scanning the surface for evidence of two small children.

By now Mum was wailing loudly which was very embarrassing, but maybe understandable; she'd just lost her boyfriend's kids. A woman standing nearby slipped her arm around her shoulder.

Woman: Don't worry, lady, we find them. The police are coming.

Trevor surfaced, along with about ten other people.

Mum: Anything?

Trevor shook his head, too breathless to speak, and immediately dived back down. In the distance, I could hear sirens. Seconds later an ambulance and two police cars screeched to a halt beside the jetty. It crossed my mind that things might have gone too far. I hadn't really thought about involving the emergency services.

Several police officers ran along the jetty. They slung their hats to one side, along with their belts, and threw themselves into the waters which were now beginning to look like Norbury Baths on a Saturday afternoon in November.

Trevor came back up again.

Trevor: They're not down there! Where can they be?

His voice was full of desperation, his face as white as the cheese in a Greek salad. I could stand it no longer.

Me: Perhaps the tide swept them up shore.

My voice sounded tight and squeaky.

Trevor: OK, yes. Elaine, wait here. I'll go and check further up.

But someone had beaten him to it. A big Greek man with an enormous stomach hanging over his trunks (*some people have no dignity*) appeared from behind the headland. He was holding the hands of two little children who were wailing loudly (*and sounding completely fake*). Thankfully, in the melée (*another victory for my thesaurus. I thought melée was a dessert*) no one seemed to notice, but me.

Trevor pulled himself onto the jetty and rushed over to them, grabbing them both. Tears were streaming down his cheeks. I was quite touched, despite the fact it was Trevor.

Trevor: Thank God you're safe! What happened?

Blue stopped sniffing and composed himself. He then launched himself into a speech worthy of the Royal Shakespeare Company (*I learnt all about them on a school trip to Stratford-upon-Avon; Poppy and I were really impressed at the way the men wore tights to stop you getting bored.*)

Blue: We jumped in, Daddy. When we came up Elaine had gone and we couldn't get out.

Trevor's eyes narrowed. My mum became flustered.

Mum: Ellie was hurt. I only left them for a second to check she was alright.

Trevor: Ellie is fifteen. Blue and Skye are eight.

Blue: We called out, but no one came. Skye got into trouble. I held onto her, but she kept going under.

For a vegetarian, he couldn't half ham it up.

Trevor: Omigod. Elaine! What were you thinking?

Mum: Trevor, I am so sorry. I don't know how this could happen. Truly, I don't.

Then came the 'six a-mum-dment', but it fell on deaf ears.

Mum: All's well that ends well.

Trevor: That's hardly the point. Come on, kids.

He pulled Skye and Blue really close to him and the three of them walked awkwardly back along the beach. Mum looked totally defeated; I felt a pang of guilt.

Mum: How's your foot?

Me: Okay, I think I just cut it on the rock. Phew! What's that smell?

We both looked down at Mum's woollen bathing costume, which

146

had long lost the fight to protect her modesty as her nipple poked through a hole in the wool. Mum pulled it up and walked slowly back to the beach.

2.30pm

Lunch – in silence.

3.30pm – Still on the beach.

Trevor and Mum have spent the afternoon arguing which is fantastic: a total result. Blue and Skye are pretending to be too scared to go into the water which has prompted Trevor to accuse Mum of scarring them for life. I throw in the fact that I am probably suffering from Post Traumatic Stress Syndrome, which I learnt about from *The Lorraine Kelly Show* when I was off sick once. I don't think Mum believes me.

4.15pm

Trevor is still in a right strop.

It doesn't matter what Mum says, he isn't listening: perfect. It's only a matter of time before they start having the 'look this isn't working out' and the 'no, it's not you, it's me' conversation. Then everything can go back to normal. Girl power will reign once again at 31 Hollis Street. I might even offer to take the bins out every once in a while to deter Mum getting any other ideas about going out with unsuitable men.

4.30pm

Things are still bad but who cares? My work is done here. It is time to turn my attention to tonight and my secret tryst (*got that from Romeo and Juliet*) with Taki. This is it. Forget second base, I think Taki is aiming for a home run and I'm in to bat.

TEXT TO POPPY:

Life's great.
Mum and Trevor are finished.
Me and Taki are on for tonight.

TEXT FROM POPPY:

Glad for you. Dad has
had the waiters arrested.
I'm grounded forever.
Will have to live life through you.
Send details.

Blimey, things are looking rough in Sorrento. At least he hasn't confiscated her mobile phone. That really would be cruel in the extreme. Mind you, Mum would chain me to a radiator if she knew (*not that the hovel has any. Plenty of leaky pipes though*).

I had just one more thing to do, just to make sure tonight

goes without a hitch. I strolled over to where George and Sophia were lying on their sunbeds.

Me: Hi.

George/Sophia: Hi!

Me: Can I ask you a favour?

George: Sure.

Me: Can you cover for me?

George: Cover?

Me: Yes, I want Mum to think I'm out with you tonight. If she asks, can you go along with it?

The two of them exchanged anxious looks.

George: I'm not sure...

God, how totally spineless. Whatever happened to teenage solidarity?

Me: Please?

George: Okay, but Ellie, be careful.

Who are you, my mother? What fifteen-year-old tells someone to be careful? I'll be careful when I'm old, say 25.

✵ ✵ ✵ ✵ ✵

7.00pm – Back in the hovel.

Mum is reading *Toxic Bachelors* by Danielle Steel (*that's more like it, girl*). Trevor has taken the savages into the village to spend some 'quality time' with them.

He has told Mum that he thinks their relationship has come between him and his kids. Mum has retaliated by saying she had had precisely the same thoughts about me and would prefer to spend the evening alone with her daughter. God, I've seen more maturity in a Year 7 PE class! Still, I can't complain, the end of their relationship is eminent (*or should that be imminent? I can never remember*). Dinner with just Mum sounds good, but I hope she turns in early, otherwise I may have some problems sneaking out to meet Taki. Now Trevor's out of the frame, she might be more vigilant.

10.00pm

Mum and I have just got back from the restaurant to find the savages are in bed with Trevor. They're all fast asleep. Mum has been relegated to the savages' room: Mum is devastated. Wow, separate rooms already – I didn't expect that quite so soon.

Mum and I had a really nice meal which reminded me of what life was like before Trevor came on the scene. Mum talked too much, which is always a sign she is really upset. But I figured as Trevor wouldn't be in our lives for much longer, the least I could do is let her get a few things off her chest.

Mum: I'll never forgive myself for what I did. I love those kids; the thought of what might have happened to them is unbearable.

Me: But they're safe Mum, nothing happened. They probably enjoyed all the attention, knowing them.

Mum: But it could have ended so differently. And now Trevor doesn't trust me with his kids. And if you don't have trust, well...

Oh no, don't cry.

Me: I am sure he'll get over it. He'll forgive you. (*I can't believe I said that. I don't want him to get over it. I want them to split up.*) Although I must admit, it's pretty bad; they are only eight.

Mum: Thanks.

Me: Sorry.

Mum: How's your foot?

Me: Better thanks. How's your rash?

Mum: Wonder how your dad and Delphine are getting on.

Wow. Mum never mentions the D word, preferring to refer to Delph as 'your dad's bit of fluff'. It was then that I noticed she was on her third Ouzo. Is this the beginning of her descent into alcoholism?

Mum: You know, I was madly in love with your father once. He used to wear this lovely midnight-blue velvet jacket and drive a gold Ford Capri. He looked like Jason King.

Jason who? Velvet?!

Mum: He was so unpredictable, Ellie. You never knew what he was going to do next? We were always laughing and joking. He used to call me Looney Lainy.

Loony Lainy? Hold on; there's nothing loony about Mum, other than her belief that every male over the age of twelve fancies her daughter.

Me: So why did you leave him?

Mum: It wasn't enough. Excitement doesn't pay the bills, Ellie. He spent all his time chasing madcap schemes while I had to go out and get a proper job to keep us all afloat. I went back to work when you were two months old. Didn't want to, couldn't afford not to. Any money I made, your dad spent.

This actually made me feel better; clearly my inability to leave Accessorize without spending at least £10 is hereditary, so there is very little I can do about it.

Mum: It seemed to me that I did all the worrying while your dad had all the fun. How bloody ironic that less than a year after we split up he goes back to college, trains to become an accountant and hitches up with a woman with breasts the size of Snowdonia (*is that really ironic, or just really bad luck?*).

Oh God, she was drunk. She had sworn *and* referred to the size of Delphine's chest in one breath. I wonder if Greece has rehab.

Mum: Now I've found myself a good, steady bloke who makes me feel alive and I've gone and blown that too.

She threw another shot of Ouzo down her neck; now I really was worried. Mum said Trevor made her feel 'alive' – he makes me feel like hibernating. We didn't seem to be talking about the same person here.

Me: Do you think Trevor will leave you?

Mum: No, no, I'm sure he will get over the fact I NEARLY KILLED HIS KIDS.

Me: Sorry.

Mum: Not your fault.

I helped her back to the hovel where she finally collapsed on Blue's bed, totally inebriated (*great word, not sure about the spelling, but forget GCSE, that has to be university level*). Now I have to worry about Mum's liver as well as her lungs.

1.00am

Everyone is asleep apart from Mum, who I think might be unconscious. This is it!!! Taki Time.

2.30am

I literally want to die...

What a total disaster. I don't know whether I should laugh, cry or just do myself in. I certainly can't ever return to Norbury, not without referring myself for therapy.

I went to the square to meet Taki. He appeared almost immediately and we headed out for the same beach as we had been to before. It was completely deserted this time, so no chance of my grandmother emerging from the dark waters.

Taki had bought a rug which was really thoughtful of him. He spread it out on the sand and we lay down on our backs.

Taki: See, look there. Ellie's star.

I looked up and there it was again, all bold and bright.

Taki leant over and started kissing me. It went on forever. A lovely, tingly sensation warmed my whole body. When he stopped, my breathing was really short (*oh God, perhaps I'm asthmatic*). I took a deep breath and tried to relax. I really didn't want this night to end with me having to blow into a brown paper bag.

Taki put his hand under my t-shirt and moved it up towards my bra. If he was disappointed to find it was underwired *and* padded, he didn't show it. He simply used the edge of my bra to guide his hand round my back to the clasp which he tugged at lightly.

I sat up.

Me: Wait.

Taki: Ees problem?

Me: Er, no.

Taki: What then?

Me: I thought I heard my grandmother.

Taki: Again? No one here, just me and beautiful Ellie. I love you.

All of a sudden I really wasn't so sure this was such a good idea. I mean, I *was* enjoying it so far but maybe I just needed more time to adjust to where we were heading. I tried to think of something to say that would slow things down a bit.

Me: What about contraception?

Genius. Even I know you have to use protection (*good to show examiner I'm aware of my social responsibilities – hang on, there's no way I'm leaving any of this in*). Mrs Duce is always getting us to chant 'put it on, before you get it on' in Sex Ed classes.

Taki: What?

Me: You know, condoms?

He shrugged and looked totally mystified. I thought for a moment and then I began to mime being pregnant by extending my hand over my stomach several times to demonstrate I had an enormous belly.

Me: You know, condoms? Pregnant? Baby?

Taki: You want baby?

Me: No, no. I don't want baby. Not yet.

Then the penny dropped and Taki grinned broadly and produced a small square foil packet from his jeans pocket.

Taki: Ees no problem.

The darkness hid my disappointment. Then another thought flitted into my mind.

Oh God, he wasn't going to ask me to put it on him, was he? We practiced doing it once in Sex Ed classes with a carrot. Mine snapped and I couldn't stop laughing. Poppy took it all very seriously and put hers on with her teeth; Mrs Duce gave her a detention.

Taki started kissing me again. I was running out of excuses. I realized I really didn't want to go through with 'it' after all – I just wasn't ready. I had never been ready. I had never really thought through what 'it' actually meant. (*Must remember to take that out, in case Miss B leaves coursework lying around and it gets read by Martin and Jamie and, God forbid, Poppy*). But what choice did I have? How could I return to school in September having not done 'it', especially as Poppy sounds like she's already into double figures? I could lie, she'd never know. I had listened enough in Sex Ed classes to have a basic grasp of what goes on and I've watched an entire series of *Sex and the City*. That should be enough, shouldn't it?

Taki began kissing my neck which felt quite pleasant and, if I'd thought that was all that he was going to, I would've let him carry on, but I could tell by the 'activity' in his jeans that it wasn't.

Me: Stop. Stop.

He stopped and actually looked quite hurt.

Taki: Why?

Me: I'm, I...I have to tell you. I'm only fifteen.

Of course, why didn't I think of that earlier? He's breaking the law and from what I've seen of the cops around here they're not to be messed with. If Trevor can get four hours for dropping a stone, God knows what the penalty is for underage sex.

Taki: It's okay. In Greece, ees no problem.

Omigod, that's all I needed, a country with lax laws. It was time to be honest. I took a deep breath.

Me: Look Taki, I'm sorry. I really like you but I've changed my mind. I can't go through with this.

Taki: But I love you.

Me: I'm sorry.

Taki: But I am man.

Me: And I am sorry.

He sighed and stroked my cheek with the back of his hand. He kissed me again. This time I froze. He seemed to be ignoring the fact I had said no. He was lying on top of me. I tried to push him off but he was too heavy.

Me: Taki, no.

Taki: It's ok. I love you.

Me: I said no!

I panicked and started slapping at him with my hands but he kept on trying to kiss me. I could feel his hand reaching down and starting to undo my jeans.

Suddenly I could hear shouting. I looked down the beach and picked out dark figure stumbling towards us in the sand. The next thing I knew, Taki was being dragged off me. I saw him stand up and swing for this stranger but the man caught his fist and sent him tumbling over onto the sand.

Stranger: Hold it right there, young man! Take your hands off her.

The voice sounded familiar. I sat up and saw Trevor. But Trevor as I'd never seen him before. His face was a mask of fury as he stood and glared down at a cowering Taki.

Taki: I do nothing.

Trevor: Too bloody right you don't. What the hell do you think you're playing at? No means no! Now get out of here and don't ever come near her again.

Taki looked as if he was going to cry. Then he ran off the beach, jumped on his moped, started it up and sped away. Trevor knelt down.

Trevor: You okay?

I noticed then that I was shaking.

Me: Fine. Thanks.

Trevor: No problem.

We walked back towards the main road.

Me: How'd you know where to find me?

Trevor: Lucky guess.

Then it dawned on me what had happened. Of all the low-life things to do to a person! Even Mum wouldn't stoop that low. Still, Trevor is a teacher; they've no concept of a person's right to privacy. I've lost count of the number of times my schoolbag has been searched.

Me: You read my coursework, didn't you?

Trevor: No.

Me: Then how?

Trevor: Let's just say it pays to know who your friends are.

It seemed like he was telling the truth. I thought for a moment.

Me: That nerd George told you, didn't he? The pig!

Trevor: The main thing is you're alright.

Me: I'm fine. I had everything under control before you arrived.

Trevor: Good.

Me: Are you going to finish with Mum?

Trevor: No, I'm not. I love her. I'm sure we can work this out.

Me: Good.

I know. I can't believe I said it myself, but I was in a weakened state: after all he had just saved my honour. Perhaps he's been practicing that reiki-mumbo-jumbo rubbish on me; he has cast a spell on me and I don't even know it. I must remember not to hold his gaze for any length of time.

We reached the road and hailed a taxi back to the hovel.

3.30am

I'm exhausted, but I can't sleep.

I'm not sure what to think about what happened on the beach. I realise I've now got less than a week to actually 'do it' but, to be honest, the whole thing is losing its appeal. I keep thinking about Taki on top of me. I could hardly breathe. Is that why people are always so breathless in the films, they're all trying not to suffocate?

Is that what 'it' is like? Maybe I'm not ready, maybe I never will be. Perhaps I'm going to have to accept that I'm on the shelf, along with Lucy Telling. Martin Hopegood was right all along, I *am* frigid. I wonder if I should go and see my GP.

But if I don't do 'it,' what will Poppy say? We made a promise to each other and now I've gone back on my word. What kind of friend am I?

Or could Poppy be wrong? Maybe I don't have 'do it' now. Maybe everyone else is lying. I don't really know what to think anymore.

DAY NINE

10.00am

Mum and Trevor are still not talking to each other.

Actually, Mum isn't talking to anyone because she has a stinking hangover. She looks terrible and is displaying all the ravages of alcohol abuse (*I must remember to get her booked into the Norbury AA when we get back. Poppy will be so impressed; her dad doesn't have a drink problem*). Trevor just looks miserable. Even Blue and Skye aren't gloating as much as I expected them to.

Not heard from Poppy which is a real worry. Perhaps her dad has confiscated her mobile phone, after all. Pig! Communication is a basic human right. I might call Childline on her behalf. Though on second thoughts, better not to get involved. Don't want to do anything that might put her dad and my mum in contact.

11.30am – At the hovel.

Trevor has taken the kids to look at a cave that was used by monks in the 11th century. Lucky them. He even took the love child – which I thought was a really generous gesture, but after he left Mum burst into tears.

Mum: See, he doesn't even trust me with our own baby.

☆ ☆ ☆ ☆ ☆

12.15pm

Mum has now gone back to bed, thank God!

I don't understand it. Trevor obviously hasn't told her about last night. If he had I'd have been packed off to a convent by now. But if not, why not? Maybe there's some secret reason – I think it's called a 'hidden agenda' (*check with Miss B*), although I'm not sure what hiding calendars has got to do with anything. So what's his game? Perhaps he's just trying to score parental points over Mum which, to be honest, wouldn't be that difficult. After all, he did look after me because my own mother was incapable through drink...

2.00pm

I got bored hanging around the hovel, so I've taken myself off to the beach.

2.15pm

Omigod, I've just seen Taki. He's sitting on the beach with some other boys. I could hear him say something like: 'little girl' as I passed.

My cheeks burned with shame. A lump formed in my throat. I hardly need Trisha to work that one out for me. He thinks I'm a total kid.

3.00pm

Even though it's baking hot and I'm rapidly turning into one big freckle, I've decided to walk back to the hovel. You never know, with any luck I'll be abducted by aliens; my life on earth is in tatters. My prospects of doing 'it' before I get back to Norbury are minus a million. In fact, I don't rate my chances of doing it before I reach 30 at the very earliest.

And to make things worse (*if that's possible*) Mum and Trevor will probably have patched their relationship up by now which means Trevor will be totally intolerable and is probably drawing up a new list of questions about the continental shelf as I write this. I bet he's told Mum about me and Taki and now she'll probably get me certified when we get back to Norbury and I'll end up in a home for wanton teenagers. 'Life's a beach!'

7.00pm

I can barely write this, my hand is shaking with excitement. It just goes to show that life is full of surprises and not all of them have to be an unscheduled, last-minute revision test.

Despite what I said before, I am I pleased I didn't get snatched by a bunch of E.T.s (*I'm not even going to attempt to spell it out, I'm bound to get it wrong and that could cost me crucial marks*).

Anyway, I walked into the hovel and found Mum sitting there, still looking bleary eyed, at the kitchen table. She was smoking a cigarette. Another smouldered in the ashtray. Wow, things are bad, I thought. She's lighting cigarettes, two at a time. Now she's trying to do herself in by giving herself lung cancer. Surely there are quicker ways of topping yourself. But then the owner of the other cigarette emerged from one of the rooms, laughing.

Me: Dad!

Dad: Ellie!

I couldn't believe it. There was my dad, standing in the middle of the hovel with a big wide grin on his face. I ran over to him and gave him a huge hug.

Me: Dad, what are you doing here?

Dad: Just thought I'd drop in and see my favourite girl.

Mum: Delphine's left him.

Me: Dad, I'm sorry.

Dad: Actually, it was me who finished with her, but no matter. 'Easy come, easy go', as they say.

Mum: Easy being the operative word.

Me: Dad, it's fantastic to see you. I've missed you so much.

Dad: It's okay, I'm here now.

Just then Trevor arrived back with the other inmates. When he saw Dad, he almost fell over with shock, although he pretended to be cool about it.

Trevor: Brian.

Dad: Trevor.

Trevor turned to Mum and smiled as he handed her a small box.

Trevor: There was a gift shop next to the cave. I bought you something.

Mum opened the box. Inside there was a small, bright blue bead with a black centre.

Mum: Thank you. What is it?

For some reason, Trevor looked straight at Dad.

Trevor: It's called an evil eye. It's to help ward off evil spirits. It only works if you receive it as a gift from another.

I wanted to say 'Careful, Mum, it could be a trick', but I didn't. In fact nobody said anything for ages. It was really embarrassing. It was a bit like our History trips with Mr. Greenaway. He's always trying to start conversations with us. Like any of us want to talk to a teacher!

Mr. Greenaway: So what type of music do you like to listen to, Ellie?

Me: Lots.

Mr. Greenaway: Have you lived in Norbury long, Ellie?

Me: Too long.

And then there's a massive pause because he can't think of anything else to say and neither can I. It's excruciating.
     Finally, Trevor broke the silence.

Trevor: Elaine, I think I'll pop into the village with Blue and Skye and get something to eat.

Mum: Okay, if you're sure. Thank you for the present, by the way, it's lovely.

Lovely? Maybe, if you're into voodoo.
   Trevor and the twins left.

Dad: So, how's life with the beatnik?

Mum: Good, thanks.

Dad: So good you're sleeping in separate beds?

Blimey, Dad's perceptive for a guy. But he has got a point; even though I prefer it when Mum and Trevor don't even sleep in the same postcode area, they are meant to be getting married and sleeping in separate bedrooms is not a good omen. Surely Mum can see that?

Mum: That's none of your business, Brian, and I have to say it really isn't on, you just turning up out of the blue like this. You could've phoned to say you were coming.

Me: I don't mind.

Dad: No, your mum's right, Ellie. To be honest Elaine, despite our differences, you've always been a good friend to me and right now I need a friend.

Mum: Just as long as that's all you're after.

I'm sure I caught a hint of a smile on Mum's face. Dad grinned.

Dad: Of course.

Whoa! What was going on here? Is it possible that Mum and Dad still fancy each other? If only Poppy was here, she'd know instantly. She's brilliant at being able to work out if there's sexual chemistry between a man and a woman. She kept telling us for ages that there was something going on between Miss Bartlett and Mr. Greenaway but none of us believed her. I mean he wears corduroys, for God's sake! And she's, well, quite trendy for a teacher. I've seen her in Monsoon a couple of times. Then Sandra Whitbread saw them snogging in his Honda Civic in the car park of the Cock and Bull pub which was a bit embarrassing really, as Mrs Greenaway takes us for Art (*remember to remove this. I don't want to be responsible for marital break ups. Could be dangerous to distract teachers from the very important job of getting me through my GCSEs*).

Is there sexual chemistry between Mum and Dad? She just seems a bit irritated by him. I'm not sure that counts.

7.50pm

Dad has checked himself into a five-star resort down on the coast. It sounds fantastic, better than this shanty town that we've ended up in. I really wanted to go with him, but I don't want Mum to feel I'm being disloyal. Besides, he never offered to take me.

Trevor and the delinquents got back from the village a little while ago. This time he's bought a protractor, a wooden carving of the Virgin Mary and a bag of self-raising flour. I wouldn't mind so much but he is actually trying to convince us that he intended to buy these things and I know for a fact that he's an atheist.

167

Someone who practices reiki certainly wouldn't be caught with pictures of Jesus' mother on them (*good to show a grasp of religion*).

Trevor: The Greek's definitely getting better. It's good to see Brian. He's looking well, isn't he?

Mum: You think so?

Trevor: Yes I do. Ellie seems pleased to see him.

Mum: Yes, she is.

Trevor: Anyone fancy a pancake?

Mum: Look Trevor, I don't...

At that point Dad strolled in, which was very bad timing on his part as I'm certain Mum was about to dump Trevor and not before time. Or perhaps she was about to give him some tips on cooking, I'm not sure. Either way, surely Dad's arrival will make her realise what she's really been missing.

Dad: Evening, campers. Anyone hungry?

Mum: Well, Trevor was about to cook.

I'm not sure making glue for papier-mâché masks can be classed as cooking (*good to show examiner I know un peu de Français as well as English*).

Dad: Come on! Let's go out and eat; my treat.

10.00pm

Just got back from dinner. It was awful. We all went to a taverna near the beach.

Dad: Still trying to save the world, Trevor?

Trevor: I like to do my bit.

Dad: You know recycling is just one big con, don't you?

Trevor: Hardly, Brian. If we don't learn to recycle our waste, the planet will become one big dustbin.

Dad: But did you know it takes more energy to recycle a can than it does to make a new one? I read it in the *Daily Mail*.

I'm not sure, but I think I sense a bit of Alpha-Male stuff happening here. Poppy told me that this a biological term for when boys show off in front of girls, like when we're lining up for Science and Jamie Harbinger and Martin Hopegood jump up and try and touch the ceiling. Apparently, it's in their genes (*I think it's too much Dr Pepper, personally*).

Somehow I didn't think Dad and Trevor were talking about recycling at all. I think their conversation was a metaphor for something else, but I'm not sure what (*I think I was away when we did metaphors*). Anyway, when we got back to the hovel, it continued.

Mum: How's work, Brian?

Great, that sounds promising. Mum is obviously trying to suss out if Dad has become more responsible with his money.

Dad: Good, very good. I'm moving into the overseas property market so I'm spending a fair bit of time abroad. Nice, Madrid,

Dubai, that kind of thing.

Wow, Dubai! It just sounds so exotic. Not like Norbury which sounds so dull. Isn't Dubai next door to Iraq?

Dad: How about you Trevor? Been on any good field trips recently?

Trevor: Yeah, we took a bunch of kids to Wales for the first time this year. It was cool.

Dad: Cool? Bet it was bloody freezing!

Dad is so funny. He really is. I've missed him so much. He's such a laugh to have around.

Dad: Well, I'd best be making a move. Trevor, any objections to me spending tomorrow with Ellie?

Trevor: Of course not, Brian. She is your daughter after all.

Typical; he's just trying to get me out of the way so he has Mum all to himself, although I would prefer to spend the day with Dad, but that's not the point.

Dad: And I'm sure you'd like your mum to come along too, wouldn't you, Ellie?

Me: That's a great idea. Mum, say you'll come with us, please.

Mum: Well...

She looked anxiously at Trevor.

Trevor: It's okay, Elaine. I was planning on taking Blue and Skye to view the site of a 4th century lighthouse.

The site? So he means it's not even there anymore? Does he realise he's condemning his kids to a life of therapy? Still, who cares; Mum, Dad and I (*or should that be Mum, Dad and me? I can never remember. Surely you don't have to know that kind of stuff to get a C grade, do you?*) are spending the day together. Oh and the love child, I suppose.

Dad: That's settled then. I'll pick you girls up tomorrow at 10.00.

11.00pm

Have gone to bed.

I can't get over Dad coming all this way to see Mum and me: I think he still really likes Mum. He must do. Maybe she still likes him. It's possible; after all, they never really fell out with each other as such. She just got fed up with him spending all her money. But he's an accountant now so he has obviously learnt the error of his ways. Maybe when Mum realises this, they'll get back together again. How amazing would it be, if Mum and Dad REMARRIED? I could be their bridesmaid: cool. On second thoughts, pastel shades make me look anaemic (*at least I think so – not totally sure what it means*).

DAY TEN

9.30am

Totally weird morning...

Mum and Trevor are still in separate beds and have barely said a word to each other. Trevor seems to blame Mum for Dad's appearance. Either that or he's really annoyed to discover she is still smoking like a chimney. (*Suppose it could still be due the fact she nearly drowned his kids.*)

11.15am

Five-star hotel. Whoopee!...

Dad's taken us to spend the day with him at the hotel resort where he is staying. It's fantastic and has got three swimming pools. A rather dishy waiter has just served me a Coke by the poolside. Things are looking up.

TEXT TO POPPY:

Ditched Taki,
v. immature.
Dad here.
At posh hotel.

Gorgeous waiter!

Mum and Dad are in the pool. Thank God, Mum isn't wearing the sheepskin rug. Dad has bought her a gorgeous, chocolate brown bikini from the hotel shop. Her rash has almost gone. They look like they are having a good time. I'm looking after the love child, who is unusually calm.

1.20pm

Wow! I don't believe what just happened. Dad has told Mum he wants to get back with her. How incredible is that?...

They got out of the pool and must have thought I had fallen asleep on my sunlounger, because Dad just started telling Mum how much he loved her and wanted her back. Mum was a bit cool, to be honest.

Mum: So what really happened between you and Delphine?

Dad: The truth? She was a nice girl, but she couldn't compare to you, Elaine.

Mum: Compare? I seem to remember that several of her bits definitely exceeded mine, Brian.

Let it go, Mum. No point being bitter. You could always have plastic surgery. I'm sure Dad would pay.

Dad: I never got over you, Elaine, you know that.

Mum: We were together a long time, Brian. And we have Ellie:

there'll always be a bond between us.

Dad: I want more than a bond, Elaine.

Mum: What are you saying?

Oh for God's sake, what do you think he's saying? What do you want him to do, beg? Give the guy a break!

Dad: What I'm saying is, I've changed. I know you don't believe me, but I have. I've grown up. It's taken a while, I know, but I'm ready to face up to my responsibilities.

Actually, I wasn't sure where he was going with this one. Perhaps he was offering to increase her child support allowance.

Mum: I don't understand, Brian.

Dad: Elaine, what I'm trying to say, very badly, is that I want you back. I want to be with you and Ellie and I want us to be a proper family again.

I wanted to shout 'Say yes, Mum! Go on!' But I didn't, and she didn't say anything either.

2.30ₚₘ – By the pool.

Dad popped back to his room after lunch to make a couple of phone calls while Mum and I stayed by the pool. I decided to seize the opportunity to try and make Mum see sense.

Me: I heard you and Dad talking.

Mum: I thought you were asleep.

Me: Well, are you going to get back together or not?

Mum: I'll always be fond of your dad, Ellie but isn't as easy as just saying yes and acting as if nothing ever happened.

I'm willing to give it a try. I don't see why you can't.

Me: Why not? He loves you Mum. Isn't that enough?

She took so long to answer me, I thought she hadn't heard.

Mum: Ellie, your Dad nearly cost us everything. And I mean *everything*: he left us totally broke, Ellie. Every time the door went, I was terrified it was the bailiffs. We only survived because GM bailed us out. I just couldn't carry on living like that any more, so I left. I know we haven't got much now and believe me, I wouldn't have chosen to live in Norbury, unless I had to, but we have enough, Ellie. We are secure, I can't jeopardize that.

Me: But he's changed, Mum; he's an accountant. If other people can trust him with their money, why can't you?

Mum: It isn't just the money, Ellie.

Me: So what then?

She didn't say anything for a while.

Mum: I didn't want to tell you this because I didn't want you to worry, but the truth is shortly after your Dad and I split, I had, well, a bit of a breakdown.

Me: Well, what do you expect if you insist on buying a ten-year-old car with 90,000 miles on the clock? I knew we should have gone for the Cherokee Jeep.

But she wasn't listening.

Mum: I hadn't been sleeping well and was worried about you. It was all getting a bit on top of me. And that's when I started going to counselling.

Wait a minute. Counselling? Omigod, I can't believe it – Mum went to a counsellor and didn't tell me! How thoughtless can you be? If the school had known my mum was a bit of a nutter, I could've got out of loads of schoolwork. I might even have been saved the misery of Year 9 SATs. I'd have got loads of sympathy, plus loads of street cred. When Sandra Whitbread said her mum couldn't attend parents nights because she was agoraphobic and had that disease where you're addicted to cleaning (*don't think I need to worry about that one*) she got out of doing homework for two months, until Mrs Duce bumped into Mrs Whitbread one Saturday morning, knee-deep in compost at the Evergreen Garden Centre where she works.

Mum: And of course that's where I met Trevor.

Now, why does that not surprise me? A man who wears hair grips must have issues and definitely needs professional help.

Mum: I could've got anyone. It was sheer chance that Trevor was allocated to me as my counsellor.

Me: Trevor, a counsellor? No way! I thought he was a Geography teacher.

I can't believe Trevor is a counsellor. What does he do, tell people to list ten things about Sri Lankan tea plantations to help take their mind off the fact that their 40-year-old husband has just run off with the au pair?

Mum: He is a teacher, but he's also a qualified counsellor and a very good one. He helped me enormously.

Me: I can see that. I thought having a relationship with your patient was illegal or something.

Mum: It's *client*, not patient if you don't mind. I was in counselling, not Broadmoor. Besides, I didn't start seeing Trevor until six months after I finished my sessions with him. We bumped into each other by accident outside Fresh and Wild in Soho.

Soho? The red-light area? Fresh and Wild? What's that, a lap-dancing club? Oh God no! Please don't tell me it's a sex shop.
    Mum clocked the look of disgust on my face.

Mum: It's an organic vegetable shop. I was just going in as Trevor was leaving. He was carrying a huge bottle of almond oil.

Mum laughed at the memory. I didn't think it was funny at all. Almond oil? That's repulsive. Does Trevor's school know what a depraved double life its Geography teacher leads?

Mum: Yes, I remember now. I'd only popped in for some oatmeal.

Oatmeal? It just gets worse.

Mum: Anyway the point is, Ellie, I'll always be fond of your dad, but that's a long way from wanting to get back with him. And then, there's Trevor to consider.

Dad: Hi girls. This looks serious. Ellie, look after the baby. Your mum and I are going jet skiing.

I walked down to the beach carrying the love child and watched them from the shore as Dad drove at the waves like a maniac. At first Mum seemed really nervous but by the end she was laughing so much she fell off, which made her laugh even more.

5.00pm

Dad and Mum are in the kitchen back at the hovel. They seem to be getting on really well. Mum's even mentioned Dad's velvet jacket. I have decided to leave them to it and go for a walk around the village. I guess I should still be looking for a guy to do it with, though, I'm not really sure I can be bothered with the whole thing anymore. Maybe I'll just check out the guy who runs the kiosk.

5.30pm

Just got back from my walk. Not even a whiff of guy-ness...

I met Trevor coming back from his day trip with the savages. Skye was chasing Blue with a dead scorpion he had found. He looks more and more like an extra from *The Lord of the Flies (we did it in Year 9: totally dull. There are no girls in it, how sexist is that?).*

Trevor: Hi Ellie, had a good day?

Me: Fantastic.

Trevor: Good. What about your mum?

Me: She had a terrific time, thanks.

Trevor: Good. Well, she can tell me all about it. Let's go, kids.

He took Blue and Skye's hands and began to walk off towards the hovel. Mum and Dad had had such a good time together, I didn't want Trevor to turn up and spoil everything, so I decided to try and stall him.

Me: Dad's still there.

Trevor: No problem.

That didn't work. I had to think of something else.

Me: Dad's asked her to go back with him and I'm fairly sure she's going to say yes.

Well, it was partly true and it was only a matter of time before it was completely true. Trevor turned pale and stared at me for a moment.

Trevor: Elaine and Brian? Together? Are you sure?

Me: As good as.

He didn't seem to know what to do. It was a bit embarrassing really. Then he muttered something about seeing us all later and wandered off towards the village with Blue and Skye in tow.

I watched him disappear out of sight. I was sure I had done the right thing. It's better that he finds out now. Still, I couldn't ignore the guilt welling up inside me as I watched him go. He looked so sad.

Back at the hovel, Mum and Dad were waiting for me. Dad wanted to go for something to eat but Mum insisted on waiting for Trevor to come back. I didn't tell her that I had seen him, I don't know why. It didn't seem the right thing to do. In the end, Dad started to get impatient.

Dad: He's probably found an old ruin or something and got held up, although I shouldn't talk about GM like that.

Mum giggled.

Mum: Brian! I think we should wait for them. They won't be long I'm sure.

✩ ✩ ✩ ✩ ✩

10.00pm

Just got back from the restaurant.

Trevor and the others never showed so we went on our own, just like when we were a family. We had a terrific time. Dad is so funny, he kept trying to order really English dishes like jellied eels and steak and kidney pie. Mum seemed to relax too; she's definitely less tense when she's allowed to smoke in public.

When we got back to the hovel, things were missing. I thought we'd been burgled, but who would steal lavender joss sticks? Then it dawned on us all that Trevor and the delinquents had taken all their stuff and gone. Mum looked a bit shocked.

Mum: I can't understand it. Why would he leave?

Dad: Perhaps Glastonbury has started. Look, I can stay if you like. Or you can check into my hotel?

Yes, great idea.

Mum: No, Brian, thank you anyway. We'll be fine here on our own. I don't understand it. Perhaps they've decided to go camping.

Dad left, leaving me and Mum on our own. Even the vile hovel felt a bit too big for us both.

Mum: Ellie, where do you think he's gone?

Me: Dunno.

Mum: I don't understand. Why would he leave so suddenly like that without saying anything to me?

Me: Dunno.

She'll thank me. One day.

DAY ELEVEN

9.00am – **Dad's five-star hotel.**

Dad has booked Mum into the beauty spa at his hotel for a facial and a massage. He has to do some work on his laptop this morning, so I've decided to go to the beach. Mum hasn't mentioned Trevor once this morning; things are looking good.

1.00pm

On the beach. No sign of Taki, thank God. Any more humiliation is likely to push me over the edge.

2.00pm

I've just spotted nerdy George coming towards me.

What a nerve! He is the last person I want to see after telling Trevor about me and Taki. Perhaps I should just ignore him.

3.00pm

Wow, that was the coolest! I'm glad I didn't ignore George after all...

George: Hi.

Me: I'm not talking to you.

George: Why not?

Me: Because you're a snitch.

He frowned and handed me a mask and snorkel.

George: Wanna come?

Me: No.

George: Go on.

Me: Okay.

No idea why I said yes.

We put them on and swam out towards some rocks. I floated on the surface watching the fish dart in and out of the reefs below us.

Then George touched my arm and nodded at a large stone. I looked at him and pulled a face. He pointed to the rock again. It was then that I noticed that clinging to it was a small octopus, its black, beady eyes fixed on us. George prodded it gently and immediately a jet of black ink shot out in indignation. We laughed so much we had to surface. We tore off our masks and trod water beside each other.

Me: That was amazing!

George grinned, pleased he had brought a smile to my face.

We got out of the water and lay down on our towels to let the sun dry us off. After a while, I turned towards him and lifted myself up on my elbow. George kept his eyes shut and I found myself admiring his even chestnut brown skin. His thick, black, swept-back hair shone in the sun.

Me: Do you like your mum's latest husband?

George: No, he's an idiot.

Sounds familiar. Clearly, having dreadful judgment where men are concerned is not unique to English women.

Me: Doesn't that bother you?

George turned onto his side and propped himself up on his elbow, facing me. When he spoke, his breath was minty, not like Taki's.

George: No, it's her life. She has every right to be happy. She's got her life. I've got mine. I want her to be happy.

Me: Right. Do you wish your mum and dad were still together?

He looked directly at me, his eyes boring into mine. For a moment I wondered if he was going to kiss me. My heart began to pound in my chest. Then he lay back down again.

George: Not really. They were miserable together.

Me: Right.

4.15pm – Back at the hovel.

Something totally weird just happened...

I left George on the beach and got back to the hovel about fifteen minutes ago. Just as I was going in, Mrs Gnome appeared outside her door. She called over to me. I tried to ignore her but she pulled a piece of paper from her skirt pocket, came over to me and shoved it in my hand.

It was a letter. I thought it might have been from Taki. It could even have been an apology; perhaps he wanted to try again.

I unfolded it quickly and read it.

My Darling E,

It couldn't be Taki, I don't think his English is up to that.

I know I should have waited to tell you in person, but I didn't want to stand in the way of your happiness with Brian. You have enough to sort out without me making things any more complicated than they need to be.
I know it's over between us, Elaine, but I wanted to thank you for the wonderful times we had together. Blue and Skye will really miss you, as will I.
Elaine, you know that I'll always love you and I'll always be here for you, if you need me. If things don't work out, I'm at the hotel in the village for two more nights and then I'm taking the twins island hopping.

Good luck, my love, you deserve to be happy.

Trevor

PS I'll call in a couple of weeks to discuss access rights for the baby.

Oh God! The letter wasn't for me, at all; it was for Mum. And it was from Trevor. I went inside the hovel. Mum wasn't back from the hotel yet so I sat at the table and stared at the letter.

I really don't know what to do. If I give her the letter, it might ruin the possibility of her and Dad getting back together. But Trevor says he loves her, which I suppose could be an important piece of information at this time. There's only one thing for it.

4.30pm

TEXT TO POPPY:

Total Crisis!
Call me.

5.00pm

Still no word from Poppy.

5.10pm

TEXT TO POPPY:

SOS!!!!!
Need to speak urgently.

5.30pm

Still nothing.

It's no good. I can't wait any longer. I need an answer.

I dial her number and get voicemail. Where is she? What am I going to do? Should I give Mum the letter or not? Maybe I could Tippex out the last paragraph where he says he will always be there for Mum.

6.00pm

The letter is under my pillow.

6.15pm

Mum's just got back.

The first thing she did was ask if Trevor had called. I couldn't bring myself to mention the letter, not until I have decided what to do with it. It's for her own good after all.

Mum's lower lip wobbled.

Mum: He's left me, hasn't he?

Me: Dunno.

Mum: How could he just walk out on me like that, without saying a word?

Me: Dunno.

Actually he said several words, but I just didn't want to tell her.

8.00pm – At the hovel alone.

Dad's taken Mum for a meal in the village. Just the two of them. I've decided to stay back, in case Poppy contacts me. I still have no idea if I should show Mum Trevor's letter.

8.10pm

TEXT TO POPPY:

NEED TO SPEAK NOW!!!

11.00pm

Mum and Dad have just got in. Mum's giggling a lot – she's clearly been at the Ouzo again. Thankfully, I don't think the winos' store in Norbury stocks the stuff, she's clearly addicted.

They sound like they're really enjoying being together. I've

definitely made the right decision not to show her Trevor's letter...I
think.

10.00am

What a fabulous, fabulous morning!...

When I got up this morning Mum was already awake. She asked me to sit down because there was something she wanted to say to me. I could tell it was serious. The last time she asked me to sit down in that tone of voice was when she found out I had forged her signature on a sick note so Poppy and I could go shopping in Croydon. I probably would've got away with it if I hadn't written that I'd caught a bout of Hepatitis C (*Poppy's suggestion*) but would probably be back in by the end of the week, if it had cleared up by then.

Mum: Ellie, I've been thinking a lot over the last couple of days.

Me: Right.

Mum: Your Dad has made no secret of the fact he wants to give our marriage another go.

Me: Right.

Mum: And I know how much it would mean to you if he and I gave it another try.

Me: Right.

Mum: And he does appear to have got himself sorted out.

Me: Right.

Mum: So, I'm going to suggest to him today that we think about going to see a marriage guidance counsellor just to see if there might be any possibility of a reconciliation.

Me: Really? That's fantastic! (*Just as long as the counsellor isn't Trevor.*)

I did what I never do, I hugged my mother. She looked a little startled. Maybe she thought I was going to assault her.

Mum: There's a long, long way to go, Ellie, and your dad and I will have to take things slowly. Very slowly but well, I guess I'm prepared to give it a shot.

Me: Er – what about Trevor?

Oh God, why did I say that? Mum's face seemed to fall a bit. She looked down at the table.

Mum: To be honest, if he can walk away from a relationship without so much as a second thought, perhaps we didn't have much of a relationship in the first place.

Me: Right.

Something about Mum's tone wasn't entirely convincing and I suddenly felt the urge to stare at the floor. But I'm definitely doing the right thing. Mum just needs a little time.

Dad arrived to take us both back to his hotel resort for the day. I really wanted to go but I thought it would be a good idea if Mum and Dad spent some time together on their own, so I told them I wanted to stay at the hovel and finish my coursework. It never ceases to amaze me how parents always fall for that.

11.00am

I'm really worried about Poppy...

I haven't heard from her for days. Perhaps she's been locked up for sexual harrassment. Perhaps she's dropped me because she's had sex with three boys and I haven't even done it with one. I knew I should've lied about Taki.

And then there's the small matter of Trevor's letter. I still don't know what to do with it; I don't like lying to Mum. Well, that's not strictly true. It's okay to lie if it's to do with schoolwork or boys because she completely overreacts when I mention either. But this? This is *lying* lying. Although come to think of it she asked me if Trevor had *called*, she didn't ask me if he had written to her or left her a note. Technically, I didn't tell any lies at all – so why do I feel so bad? Besides, if she's back with Dad it doesn't matter if she sees the letter or not. Does it?

It's no good, I'm desperate to speak to Poppy, but she's not answering her phone, which I suspect could be at the bottom of Lake Garda (*Italian lake. Don't even know how I know that. Maybe Trevor mentioned it once. Either way, should impress the examiner*).

11.10am

I've had an idea.

Dad's left his laptop on the table. If it has an internet connection, I can email Poppy. She has a Hotmail account and probably checks it at least two or three times a day.

11.20am

I turned Dad's laptop on and clicked on to his email. It was password protected. I tried Elaine: no joy. Ellie: no joy. Delphine: that worked. I'm surprised Dad kept her as a password. Anyway, I was in. I went into his mail and clicked on new message to Poppy.

Hi Poppy,

If you get this, please reply or text me. It's all gone crazy here. Dad's back. Trevor's moved out, but still loves Mum. It's like an episode of Emmerdale *(without cows). Need to talk.*
Also had sex with man at kiosk. Need to check something with you.

Love

Ellie.

That should do it, Poppy won't be able to resist me asking her advice about a sexual matter. It's her forte (*more Italian. Perhaps the examiner will think I'm multilingual*).

I clicked the send button and Poppy's email disappeared. I was just about to turn off the computer when I noticed three unopened emails in Dad's inbox:

Viagra Max: prescription renewal.

Blimey, I didn't know Dad had a heart condition. Perhaps I should tell Mum. It might make her try harder, if she thinks his days are numbered.

Delphine: Re:

Oh no, an email from Delphine. She probably wants to get back with Dad. Perhaps I should delete it. I like Delphine, but she, like Trevor, needs to accept that Mum and Dad are meant to be. I clicked on her email:

Brian,

I'm not interested in your excuses. What you did is unforgivable.
That money was for my breast reduction op. You're lucky I don't call the police.

Delphine.

What on earth is she going on about? What money?

Allan Hallwood: Urgent!

I clicked on the last email:

Dear Mr Foster

As you have not replied to any of our correspondence, I have been left with no choice but to email you.
In the absence of any attempts to repay the outstanding loan for work carried out on the Il Picola timeshare apartments in Alicante, we have taken the difficult decision to foreclose on your business and arrange for it to go into receivership.

Please contact me immediately to discuss.

Allan Hallwood.

Foreclose? Receivership? Oh God, I wish I'd paid more attention in Business Studies. It sounded serious whatever it was. Still, I'm sure Dad had it all in hand.

I turned off the computer. I wish I hadn't looked at Dad's emails now. Delphine is obviously off her head (*she must be, what woman in their right mind wants to make their boobs smaller?*) and I didn't understand the other email at all.

12.15pm

I can't hang around all day waiting for Poppy to call. I've decided to go to the beach.

3.00pm

OH MY GOD – WHAT HAVE I DONE???...

I went to the beach. Taki was there. I should have left there and then, but I didn't want to let him scare me off the beach. He was snogging the face off another girl. Perhaps he was trying to play mind games. Poppy and I read about them in *Cosmo*. Apparently, it's when a boy fancies you but messes with your mind by going out with someone else. Poppy says Ben Hardy is always playing mind games with her. He's been out with three different girls when in fact he really wants to be with Poppy.

Either way he was wasting his time. The only game I wanted to play with him at that moment was how hard I could knee him between the legs.

Then I heard familiar voices. I looked across the bay and spotted Trevor, Blue and Skye crouching by the rocks.

Trevor: No Blue, we can't take hermit crabs back home and put them in a tank. They must be left in their natural habitat. It's important not to upset the planet's sensitive ecological balance. Plus they'll die.

At that point, Trevor spotted me and waved. He ambled over. He looked a bit pale, with shadows under his eyes. I guessed he wasn't getting much sleep, but he still managed a smile. I smiled back at him and he looked a bit surprised.

Trevor: Oh, hello Ellie.

Me: Hello.

Trevor: How are you?

Me: Good.

Trevor: Er how's your mum?

Me: Good.

Trevor: She's not mentioned anything to you about me, has she?

Me: No.

Trevor: Right.

An embarrassing silence followed, but Trevor didn't seem to want to leave and with Taki and the girl rolling around in each other's arms in the sand nearby, I was in no real hurry for him to go either.

Me: Where are you staying?

Trevor: At the hotel in the village, just until we can get things sorted. We're leaving in a few days.

Me: Trevor, can I ask you something?

He perked up.

Trevor: Sure.

Me: What does 'foreclose' and 'receivership' mean?

Trevor: Er, it usually refers to a business that has gone bankrupt. Why?

Me: Business Studies coursework.

He rolled his eyes.

Trevor: Coursework, never ends, does it? Skye, take that seaweed out of your mouth!

Trevor rejoined Blue and Skye by the rocks. They moved further up the beach out of earshot but I barely noticed. I was trying very, very hard not to throw up. My head spun so much it ached. OH MY GOD. I couldn't believe it, Dad was bankrupt. He hadn't got any money at all. He even stole money from Delphine who is lumbered with having breasts the size of Snowdonia forever. He lied to us. He'd come all this way to lie to us.

And what about Mum? Panic squeezed my windpipe so tight I could barely breathe. She was probably telling Dad right at that very moment that she wanted to give their relationship another go. She doesn't have a clue he's skint.

She can't go back to him now. If she did, it would send her over the edge, she'd have another breakdown for sure. She'd end up in a home and I'd end up homeless and smelling of wee. Would

I deserve it? Was it mostly my fault? This was terrible, I had to stop it.

10.30pm

The worst, worst day of my whole, sorry life.

By the time I got back to the hovel, Mum and Dad were sitting at the table holding hands. My stomach flipped at the very sight of them and my mouth had that weird salty taste you get just before you chuck up. I swallowed hard. I wanted to shout at her 'Stop, don't go through with it, he's broke and he'll make you broke too' (*and me, for that matter*), but their contented looks stopped me in my tracks.

Dad: Ellie, great, you're here. We've got some news for you.

Mum was smiling coyly.

Mum: I said yes, Ellie. Your dad and I are going to try and give it another go.

I looked from one to the other. I was rooted to the spot. I just didn't know what to say.

Me: Right.

Mum rolled her eyes.

Mum: Well, you could look a little more pleased about it. I thought it was what you wanted.

Dad chuckled.

Dad: Teenagers! There's no pleasing them, is there?! Anyway, we thought we'd celebrate in style. I've booked a table at the hotel restaurant tonight, which means we have to get our gladrags on. I've already bought a little something special for your mum to wear; now it's your turn, Ellie. I'm taking you shopping right now. Come on, cheer up, it might never happen.

Why do adults say that? If I look like I'm drowning in my own misery, then the chances are it has already happened and they're too late.

Dumbly, I followed Dad out to the car and got in. I was still feeling dazed, like the time Clarissa Dobson whacked me over the head with a hockey stick (*is it too late to press charges? I'm sure it was deliberate. She probably knew then that my coursework would be loads better than hers and cracked under the pressure*). Everything had gone fuzzy and I couldn't work out where I was even though I could see the school and everyone kept telling me my name and that.

Anyway, I knew we were heading towards a nearby town to buy clothes for me, which is normally my idea of heaven but I felt very uncomfortable that Dad was probably spending Delphine's boob job money on me and Mum.

Dad: You're quiet, Ellie. It's a lot to take in, I know, but it's great news, isn't it? We'll be a family, once again.

No we won't. We'll be a disaster waiting to happen. Mum will go back to worrying that the bailiffs are going to come round and I'll have to go on the free meals register at school. That was it. I couldn't stand it any longer.

Slowly I regained control over my senses. I knew what I had to do. The question was, could I do it?

I stared ahead, out of the windscreen, I couldn't bear to look at him. I took a deep breath. I had to get it out in one sentence in case it didn't come out at all.

Me: I borrowed your laptop to email my friend Poppy.

Dad: No problem.

Me: There were three emails on it for you; one from your doctor, one from Delphine and one from the bank.

Dad frowned and glanced at me.

Dad: You had no business going into my mail, Ellie. Did you say there was one from my doctor?

Me: I know you stole off Delphine, Dad. I know you're bankrupt. That's why you're here, isn't it? You're not really interested in Mum or me, you just want her money.

Dad: That's not true. You're just a kid Ellie, you don't understand. I just need a few extra grand, just to get these flats in Spain finished and then we'll all be rolling in it. Your mum understands that.

Me: So you've told her?

Dad glanced out of his side window.

Dad: Not *exactly*.

Me: Dad, you can't do this to her. It's not fair.

Dad: But you want us to get back together again, don't you?

Me: Not like this, no.

Dad: Ellie, you're overreacting. It's not as bad as you make it sound. Your mum and I have just got back together. It's what you wanted. Nothing else matters; don't spoil things.

He was trying to make light of the situation, but his voice was strained.

I risked a brief glance. His face was hard, unreadable and he was staring straight ahead, concentrating on the road. I didn't know if I had the strength to do what had to be done. The minutes drifted by. The longer I waited the harder it would be. We reached the outskirts of the town. I inhaled sharply, gathering every gram of courage I had. I closed my eyes, pictured the words in my mind and read them out aloud.

Me: Dad, I think you should go. I think you should leave Mum and me alone.

I opened my eyes and waited. He didn't say anything for ages. Then he nodded very slowly and deliberately.

Dad: You're right.

The car screeched to a halt. Dad swung the car around and we drove back to the hovel in silence. I looked out of the window and fought the tears all the way back.

Dad pulled up at the top of our road and I got out. He wound his window down.

Dad: Don't tell your Mum, Ellie.

And with that, he disappeared from our lives in a cloud of dust. I turned towards the hovel, dreading what would happen next.

I heard Mum first. She was gently humming *Dancing Queen*. I found her in the kitchen; she was already dressed in anticipation of her big night out.

She looked lovely in a slinky, ankle-length red dress. I couldn't remember the last time I had seen her in something that didn't have the dimensions of a circus tent. I gulped.

Mum saw me and her face lit up.

Mum: Hello darling. That was quick. Couldn't you find anything you liked?

I wanted to pause that moment forever. I didn't want to burst her bubble, but I knew I had to.

Me: Mum, sit down a minute. I have to tell you something.

The smile faded from Mum's face and the woman in red lowered herself into a chair. I slid into the chair opposite her; I think she knew what was coming but still had to hear it.

Mum: What is it?

Me: Mum. Dad's gone. He, er, got called away on urgent business.

I instantly regretted bottling it, it just confused her.

Mum: What? Without telling me? Well, when's he coming back?

Oh no. I was hoping she wouldn't push me for details. After all, I had about a nanosecond (*good to show a grasp of Maths – even under extreme duress*) to come up with the 'called away on business' line. I knew I had to tell the truth.

Me: He's not, Mum, he's gone for good. He told me to tell you he'd made a mistake, that you're better off without him. I'm sorry Mum, I really am sorry.

It was ages before she spoke. I wondered if I should leave her on her own for a while, but then she heaved a heavy, loaded sigh. She laid her hand on my arm.

Mum: It's not your fault, Ellie; maybe it's for the best. I'm sorry Ellie, I know how much you wanted us to get back together.

Mum slopped Ouzo into a pint glass and downed the lot in one go. Uh-oh (*note to me: from now on hide all alcohol*).

Mum: What is it with men, Ellie? Why do they keep leaving me?

Me: To be fair, you left Dad first.

Mum: But what about Trevor? I thought we had something special, Ellie, I really did. But when Brian arrived, it was like he didn't want to know me anymore. One minute we were getting married and the next he disappears into thin air, without so much as a by your leave. I thought he'd fight harder for me. (*By your leave? Sounds like it could be Shakespeare. I'll leave it in.*)

Mum took a swig of Ouzo, straight from the bottle. She's obviously spiralling out of control; Dad only left five minutes ago!
Mum smoothed the label on the bottle.

Mum: I don't think he really forgave me for nearly drowning his kids and who can blame him? I'm a sham of a mother.

Me: No, you're not. You're a good mother, most of the time.

Mum smiled weakly.

Mum: Well, that's just as well because it looks like it's just you and me now, Ellie. Girl Power!

She punched the air limply and we both sat at the table in silence.

11.00pm

Mum's gone to bed. I think I can hear her crying, but I'm not sure.

11.30pm

I can't sleep.

There are so many thoughts whirring around in my head: Dad leaving, Trevor's letter, Delphine's breasts *(perhaps I really am bisexual)* and Mum in her blood red dress, looking utterly desolate *(knew I could count on my trusty thesaurus to come up trumps, even in these trying times)*.

11.45pm

That's it, I'm going for a walk.

DAY THIRTEEN

1.00am

Can't sleep, due to what has just happened...

After Mum went to bed I sneaked out of the hovel, which was totally unnecessary as Mum was snoring so loudly it almost lifted the roof.

I didn't know where I was going, but I found myself in the village square so I bought myself a Coke from the kiosk and sat on the low wall next to it. So much had happened in the last couple of days that I just needed to sit quietly and get my head around everything.

Dad was gone. Trevor was gone. Mum and I were on our own once again and neither of us seemed very happy about it.

I slowly became aware of a large group of boys laughing and shouting nearby. I looked up. A couple of them were pointing at me and smirking. How rude! Pointing would get you knifed in Norbury.

In the middle of the gang I spied the tall figure of Taki. He had a huge grin on his face, lapping up the vile comments his friends were making about me. With everything going on it shouldn't have bothered me, but it did. Big time.

I thought about that night Trevor caught me with Taki. Why did I hold back? 'Doing it' couldn't be that difficult. Poppy had conquered half of Sorrento's hotel staff and all I'd managed was a quick fumble before being interrupted by my Mum's boyfriend. I still wasn't sure whether I was pleased Trevor turned up or not, but something about the way Taki had just looked at me told me it was best that I never found out what would have happened if he hadn't. It was all so confusing. Maybe Martin Hopegood was right: I was a sexual misfit.

George: Hello!

His cheerfulness made me jump. But inexplicably, his cheerful tone made me want to hug him. I didn't, obviously. With clothes on, he looked almost hunky. Ish.

Me: George!

George: In the flesh. Well in the bone, anyway.

He looked from me to Taki and his mates.

George: Forget them, Ellie. They're idiots.

Me: Thanks.

He sat down next to me.

George: I saw a man go into your villa. Your Mum has a new boyfriend?

I wished everyone would stop calling it a villa; they're fooling no one.

Me: No, that was my Dad, my real Dad.

George: Your dad is back? That's great news.

Me: Not really and besides, he's gone again.

George: That's too bad.

Me: No, it was a good thing, in the end.

George: So why are you still sad?

Me: Dunno.

He jumped up and held out his hand.

George: I know what'll cheer you up, Ellie. Come on, I'll show you something special that'll make you smile.

I took George's hand and he led me to his moped; I hesitated. After all, I was still paying a heavy price for the last time I disappeared off on the back of a boy's moped. Though, to be honest, even if he did try something I quite fancied my chances against him. He wasn't much taller than me and he certainly wasn't as wide: I've seen thicker cord. Although I reckon George could be quite good looking, if he ate more.

George: It's okay. We're not all like Taki, you know.

He smiled again. Something warm spread through my chest.

George: Hey, you want to drive?

Me: Erm, that's probably not a good idea.

George: It's easy. I'll show you how.

He talked me through the moped which seemed a lot less complicated than my hair straighteners. (*Dear examiner, FYI, George said it is totally legal for fifteen-year-olds to ride mopeds in Greece.*)

When he had finished, I climbed into the saddle, flicked the stand up and turned the key in the ignition. The front headlight came on and, like a persistent mosquito, the moped hummed into life. George slipped into the seat behind me and wrapped his arms around my waist.

George: Okay, let's go.

Me: Where to?

George: The beach, of course.

I opened the throttle thingy (*no idea what this is so I can't really claim extra marks for mechanical knowledge*). The bike shot forward and wobbled dangerously. George and I lurched backwards, but just managed to hang on.

Me: Sorry.

I tried the throttle thingy again and this time we set off slightly more smoothly. Within minutes we were swerving through the dark bumpy streets. I could hear George laughing in my ear. And I laughed too.

When we hit the open road, my T-shirt billowed as the wind whooshed past my face, ruffling my hair. It felt like we were flying through the night. Thank God no one could see me because I had a horrible feeling I was grinning like a maniac. How come people get road rage when driving is such fun?

I looked over my shoulder at George.

Me: This is so cool.

George: That's good, but you need look at the road, not me.

I turned to face the front. In the headlight I could see we had begun to veer towards an open field. I quickly righted the bike and we continued on the road.

Me: Sorry.

George squeezed my waist and laughed.

George: Stop apologising.

A few minutes later, we pulled up at the beach where I have spent most of my days since we arrived. For the Greeks it was still early and music and laughter drifted from the tavernas at the far end of the bay, almost drowned out by sound of the cicadas.

We got off the moped. I cut the engine and pulled it up onto its stand.

George: You're a natural; you should get your own moped.

Me: You are joking aren't you? My mum wouldn't even let me have a pair of Heelys when they came out, not that I'd be seen dead in them now.

George frowned.

Me: Never mind. It's not important. So why am I here?

I looked at George, waiting for an explanation but he just grinned and marched off across the sand stopping just short of the water's edge, where he stood and stared out to sea.

I joined him and followed his gaze. The sea and the sky seemed to merge into one, it was hard to work out where one ended and the other began. It was quite interesting, but hardly special.

I was about to mention this to George when I realized he was taking his clothes off; I thought he said he was different to Taki.

Me: Now, hold on a minute!

George stepped out of his trousers. Oh God, not again. I looked away. It was a long walk back to the village.

George: What? You can't go swimming with your clothes on.

Me: Swimming? I thought you were going to show me something special.

He tugged his shirt over his head.

George: I am, but it's in there.

He tilted his head towards the sea. I strained to see what he was referring to, but there was nothing there, just the dark waters.

George: Come on, Ellie. It'll be worth it, I promise.

And then he ran full-pelt into the water and dived in before surfacing in a pool of foam. He beckoned me to join him.

Sod it! I may as well join him, I thought. So I took off my shorts and shirt and ran into the cool water. I caught him up and we swam out until we could only just touch the bottom. We trod water for a few minutes, any longer and he'd have had to call Air Sea Rescue: I was exhausted.

Me: Well?

George: Look down, but keep your arms moving.

I did as I was told (*for a change*) and stared down into the black waters. I gasped in astonishment. I was bathed in a golden sheen that lit up my arms and legs. It felt like I was floating in the night sky. As I moved my hand through the water, a thousand million stars trailed in its wake.

Me: Wow! What is it?

George grinned.

George: It's phosphorescence. Incredible, isn't it?

Me: Phos for what?

George: Phosphorescence. It's caused by millions of microscopic single-celled organisms that emit a minute light when they're disturbed. (*Can I put this towards my Science coursework which I haven't done either? Must check with Mrs Duce.*)

Me: It looks like fairy dust.

I know that sounds cheesy, but it did.

I swam quickly away from George and slowed to look back to see tiny sparks shooting from my arms and legs. George caught me up and splashed me with water, only it wasn't water, it was liquid gold.

We swam, we tumbled, and we ducked and dived into the water, every one of our movements wrapped in a thick, golden blanket. I could've stayed in the sea all night, but the cold began to get the better of us and we returned to the shore.

We sat on the beach and let the cool breeze dry us before putting our clothes back on. A shiver passed through me. George put his arm around my shoulders and rubbed my arm.

Me: Thanks, George. You were right, that was special. It was amazing. Better than drugs (*joke!*).

He ran his free hand through his wet hair and grinned.

George: Not bad for a geek?

I was embarrassed that he seemed to know the nickname I had given him.

Me: No, not bad for a geek.

I don't know what came over me but I kissed him on the cheek. I don't know why, it just seemed the right thing to do. I didn't fancy him or anything like that. At least I didn't think I did. I just liked his company.

George pulled back, pretending to be offended.

George: Hold on, I'm not just your plaything, you know.

I laughed.

Me: So what are you going to do about it?

His eyes were full of teasing.

George: At the very least, I should be allowed to kiss you back and then we're evens. It's only fair.

I shrugged as if I didn't care. But actually, my heart was going crazy.

Me: Okay.

His lips met mine in a soft, gentle, undemanding kiss. No tongues, but who cares? This was miles better.

Finally he pulled away and began pulling his clothes back on.

George: Do you feel better now?

Me: Yes, I do.

George: But still sad?

I thought for a minute.

Me: Maybe.

My stomach was knotted with dissatisfaction. Something wasn't right.

George brought me back to the hovel. We whispered our goodnights to each other and he kissed me on the cheek.

And here I am. I can't sleep. I keep thinking about George. There's no way I fancy him but he's a nice guy and quite a good kisser. For a geek.

12.30pm

My life has just changed, forever...

Woke up at eleven to the smell of salt on my skin and in my hair from my trip to the beach the night before. It put a smile on my face. It didn't last.

When I emerged from my cell, Mum was already in the kitchen, sitting at the table, taking incredibly long drags on her cigarette *(hasn't she seen the Department of Health ads about passive smoking?)*. Her eyes were red and her face looked thin and drawn which, under any other circumstances, she would have been chuffed to bits with, as cheekbones are very 'in'. She was so preoccupied with her thoughts, absent-mindedly turning her lighter over and over again in her hand that she didn't even notice me. I stood and looked at her. In that instant, I knew what I had to do even though I was likely to be grounded for infinity and beyond.

I went back into my bedroom and returned a few seconds later.

Me: Mum, I have something for you. Trevor gave it to Mrs Gnome, who thought it was for me. I didn't mean to read it and I'm sorry I didn't give it to you before.

I handed her Trevor's letter. She read it; I braced myself for the hell that was about to follow. The anger that I had kept the letter from her, the fury that I had read a letter that wasn't meant for me. Oh and the usual threats about never being allowed out after seven o'clock ever again. But she said nothing. Instead, silent tears trickled down her face. Finally she looked up at me. There wasn't a trace of rage in her eyes, just crushing defeat. It was over, I had won. I had got what I wanted, which was to get rid of Trevor for good. So how come it didn't feel like a victory? How come I felt like the one who had lost badly?

Me: Right Mum, get the baby, we're leaving.

I dashed outside. Still in a trance (*I'm definitely hiding the Ouzo. although it seems to make her quite docile, which could be good thing*), Mum picked up the love child and trailed after me.

I knew there was no time to waste. I banged on next door's hovel and Mrs Gnome answered, closely followed by George.

Me: George, it's all wrong.

George blushed.

214

George: It was only a swim. And you kissed me first, remember?

I threw a worried glance at Mum but she didn't react. She just stared into the distance with lifeless eyes. *(Perhaps this Ouzo stuff affects the hearing too.)*

Me: No. My mum, my dad – it's wrong. She loves Trevor. She should be with Trevor. But he's leaving today, I have to stop them. Can I borrow your moped?

George: Sure.

Me: Get on the back, Mum.

At this point, unfortunately, the effects of the Ouzo seemed to wear off and Mum snapped out of her hypnotic state. She stared at me in horror.

Mum: I'm not getting on the back of that thing. It's a death trap! Besides, you don't know how to drive.

Honestly, woman, I'm trying to do the right thing here.

Me: Just get on the back Mum, we're running out of time.

George: Don't worry, Mrs Foster, Ellie is a great driver, I taught her myself.

Mum: What? When?

George: Last night, when we went to the beach.

Mum: Oh my God, my daughter's turned into a tearaway!

I should be so lucky.

Me: Mum, we don't have time for this. Please just get on or we'll miss Trevor. He's leaving today.

Mum's jaw dropped open.

Mum: *You* want to stop Trevor leaving? Why?

Me: Because he loves you and you love him. Now, can we go?

The corner of Mum's mouth lifted into what I think was a smile (*either that or she had just belched*). Something caught in my throat.

For the first time ever, Mum did what I asked. She climbed on behind me and hugged my waist for dear life, the smell of Ouzo wafting over my shoulder.

Mum: Do not, under any circumstances, go over ten miles an hour, that way when we crash we're likely to get away with just minor injuries.

Me: If we crash it's because you're holding me too tightly and I've passed out. Now back off.

Mum loosened her grip slightly. I turned on the ignition and the moped sparked into life. George leant forward and kissed my cheek, wishing me good luck. Mum glared at him.

Mum: She's only fifteen you know, and young for her age at that.

Oh God, even when I'm trying to sort out her love life, she's totally embarrassing me. I opened the throttle-thingy and we darted forward. Mum's arm clamped tightly around me.

George: Wait! The baby!

With all the drama, we'd both totally forgot Mum still had the love child in her other arm, crammed in between our bodies. I braked suddenly and he ran over to us.

George: Perhaps it would be better if my grandmother looks after the baby till you get back.

George threw me a sheepish grin. Clearly he wasn't *that* confident in my ability to control the moped.

Mum: Goodness. Yes, that's probably sensible.

She handed the baby to George and we set off again.

Me: I can't breathe, Mum, let go of me!

Mum: Slow down, Ellie. You're driving like a maniac!

At that point I looked down to see a little girl on a tricycle speed past, grinning up at us.

Me: If I go any slower, Mum, we'll fall over. And keep still, you're making the moped wobble.

Mum: It's not me, it's your driving. Typical teenager, blame everyone else but yourself.

We veered from one side of the narrow road to the other until finally we reached the hotel in the village.

I stopped and turned the ignition off. Mum got off and stood, looking lost, on the pavement.

Mum: Ellie, I don't think I can face him. You go.

I lifted the bike onto its stand.

Me: Okay. Wait here.

I ran into the lobby shouting for Trevor. An unshaven man in a string vest appeared from behind a counter and waved towards the door.

Man: Gone! Gone!

Oh no, this was terrible news! I raced back outside and leapt (*I know, I don't normally do leaping, but I had a relationship to save*) back onto the moped and switched it on.

Me: Quick, get on. They've already left, they must be catching the ferry.

Mum hopped on behind me. I revved the engine.

Me: Hold on, Mum, I'm going to have to step on it.

I gripped the handlebars tightly and leant forward, giving it full throttle. Nothing happened. The engine was running, but we weren't moving. I tried again; the moped roared loudly, but we stayed exactly where we were.

Me: Oh God, the moped's busted!

That was it. It was all over. There was no way we could get to the port in time to stop Trevor leaving. I had failed. I shouted above the noise of the engine.

Me: I'm sorry Mum, I really am! I tried, I really did.

Still clasping my waist, Mum leant over the side of the bike and I wondered if she was going to vomit. The news that she had missed Trevor was obviously too much for her to bear, that and the bucket of Ouzo she'd drunk.

Mum: I'm no expert, Ellie, but don't you have to take this thing off its stand if you want it to go forward?

I looked down. The wheels of the moped were suspended about five centimetres above the ground and were whizzing around happily.

Me: Yeah, I knew that.

I pushed the bike hard, the stand flicked up and finally we shot forward, spewing dust behind us. Before long we had left the village and were swerving along the open road towards the port. I'd like to think we were doing at least 80 but judging by how long it took to overtake a man on a donkey, I don't think we got passed twenty miles an hour. I only hoped we'd be there in time.

We came to a halt on the harbourside and I switched off the engine. The place was teeming with tourists boarding the dozens of different ferries.

My heart sank. I would never find Trevor and the savages in amongst this lot, but I had to try.

Me: Stay here, Mum. It'll be quicker if I go on my own.

Mum: Find them, Ellie, please.

I ran up and down the quayside, scanning the faces of the people waiting to board the different boats. Then I spotted a weedy ponytail. It was Trevor. I grabbed him by the shoulder and swung him round, but it wasn't Trevor; it wasn't even a man.

I was running out of people and it was beginning to dawn on me that I was too late. Trevor and the evil twins must have caught an earlier ferry. Dejected, I decided to return to Mum and the moped. She would be devastated and it's all my fault. How could I have been so stupid, so selfish. Trevor's gone, gone forever...

Trevor: Ellie? What are you doing here?

And there he was, about three feet from me.

Me: Oh, hi.

Trevor: Ellie, what is it, what's wrong?

I didn't really know what to say, mainly because I was still trying to catch my breath from having sprinted (*remember to remove, in case Mr Stacey gets any ideas about picking me for the athletics team*) the twenty metres from George's moped to the boat.

Me: Everything. You can't leave now, you...you...and Mum are meant to be together.

Trevor gripped the rail of the gangplank.

Trevor: Ellie, your mother has made it clear that she wants to make a go of it with your dad. I have to respect her decision.

At the top of the gangplank, the ferry captain stared expectantly at Trevor.

Ferry captain: Sir, are you boarding or not?

Me: No you don't! Look, Dad's gone and Mum wants to be with you, she always has.

Trevor: But us being together makes you miserable, I see that now. I just didn't want to admit it. I thought you'd come round.

Ferry Captain: Sir, you must get on the ship, or get off it, you can't stand on the gangway. We're leaving.

Me: No, you being with Mum doesn't make me miserable. Well, actually yes it did but it shouldn't have done and certainly shouldn't stop you two being together. Besides, you make her happy and Mum has every right to be happy. Please Trevor, Mum needs you and...and so do I. You were there for me when I really needed you, I can see that now.

Trevor: Well....

Ferry captain: Sir, leave or I call the police.

Trevor looked down at Blue and Skye.

Blue: I miss Elaine.

Skye: I miss Ellie.

Really? Actually, Skye's quite sweet – just easily led. Trevor hesitated for a second.

Trevor: Okay, let's go.

He grabbed their hands and the three of them charged off down the gangplank and leapt onto dry land.

Ferry captain: Thank God. Now we go. Crazy English!

Trevor shot a look at the Captain.

Trevor: Malaka.

Just then Mum appeared. Mum and Trevor looked at each other for ages. It was like a scene out of *Dr Zhivago*, a really boring film that Mum made me watch because I'm doing the Russian Revolution in History, which is even more boring because there isn't even any romance in it. Poppy reckons Lenin was a eunuch. I agreed, mainly because I don't know what a eunuch is, but I didn't want Poppy to know I didn't know.

Finally Mum spoke.

Mum: Trevor, please don't go, I love you.

Me: See, Trevor, I told you.

The two of them fell into each other's arms. They held each other really tightly and then snogged for ages. Oh God. Blue put his fingers down his throat and mimicked someone puking until he pushed them down too far and puked for real.

DAY FOURTEEN

1.00pm – On the beach.

The savages are playing with their evil eyes, holding them onto their foreheads pretending to be Cyclops. Trevor is trying to tell the time by putting a stick in the sand and working it out by the shadow it casts. Why doesn't he look at his watch, like everyone else? Mum and I are sunbathing.

Mum: Are you sure you're okay with all of this? You know, Ellie, I can't continue to see Trevor without your blessing.

Blessing? I'm not a priest, for God's sake.

Me: Mum, I'm fine with it, but...

Mum: But what?

Me: Promise me you won't wear that awful sheepswool bathing costume anymore. You can see your nipples.

Mum: Right.

Me: And that poncho with the orange and black zigzags and pom poms.

Mum: Right.

Me: And that purple kaftan with the huge black eye on the front.

Mum: Right.

☆ ☆ ☆ ☆ ☆

10.00pm

Just been sitting outside the hovel with Trevor. I think we have come to what is known as 'an understanding'.

Trevor: What about this one, Ellie? Where are the Andes?

Me: I think you should know, Trevor, that I dropped Geography last year. Sorry I didn't mention it before.

Trevor: It's okay. I sort of guessed.

Me: Can I ask you something?

Trevor: Sure.

Me: How did you know where to find me that night I went to the beach with Taki?

Trevor tapped his nose

Trevor: I just followed my instincts.

Me: Did Poppy's dad call you?

He thought about denying it and then changed his mind.

Trevor: Yes. Actually, he called your mum but luckily I answered the phone.

Me: What did he say?

Trevor: Just that you might have arranged to meet a boy and that he was a bit worried about you.

Me: Me? What about Poppy? He should be more worried about her. She's slept with half of Sorrento.

Trevor sighed and thought for a bit.

Trevor: Well, that's just it. Poppy hasn't slept with an Italian waiter, or any other waiter.

Me: I don't understand. What d'you mean?

Trevor: Poppy has what is commonly known as a fertile imagination. In other words she made it all up. Her dad phoned because he was really concerned that you would believe her stories and do something you might regret.

I couldn't quite believe it. Not Poppy. Why would someone as beautiful, sexy, and as popular as Poppy make stuff up? I thought I was the only one that did that. No wonder she's not replied to any of my texts.

Trevor: Don't be too angry with her.

But I didn't feel angry at all, just really let down. You know what? I don't think she got off with Ben Hardy from the sixth form at that disco, after all. In fact, I reckon I've gone further with a boy than she has. I'm not sure I want to be friends with her any more. Maybe by September I'll have forgiven her and anyway, Lucy Telling is actually quite nice. She let me borrow her Drama coursework once (*not to copy or anything. I just wanted to check I had written the questions down right*). I'm sure I could recommend a good dentist to get her teeth sorted out.

Me: I still don't understand how you knew I was on that beach.

Trevor: GM happened to mention to me that she'd bumped into you there.

Me: And you didn't tell Mum?

Trevor: Some things are best left unsaid.

I looked at him and felt strangely calm as if everything would be right with the world. (*Perhaps there's something in this reiki-voodoo thing after all.*) I got up.

Me: Think I might go inside, it's getting cold.

Trevor: Ellie?

Me: Yeah?

Trevor: Thanks.

I think I've spent too much time in the sun. My cheeks suddenly started to really burn.

DAY FIFTEEN

1.15pm – The flight home.

Totally, totally depressed. I've just said goodbye to George at the airport; I cried buckets. Last time I wept that much was when Steps announced they were splitting up (*I was only six*). Being in love is almost as miserable as not being in love.

At least George and I got to spend my last day together. It was too precious to waste time doing coursework (*surely I've written enough, even with all the personal/incriminating/illegal bits taken out?*).

George borrowed his granddad's motorboat and together we explored the coves and inlets along the coast. Then he took me to a cave with inky blue water and we spent the afternoon diving in and ducking each other. Every so often, George would slide his arms around me and plant a kiss on my lips as if it was the most natural thing in the world.

Last night, I took everyone to the beach to show them that phosphorescence stuff. Trevor was dead impressed, he had no idea they had it here. Ha, call yourself a teacher! Blue and Skye tried to catch the stars in their fishing nets. Mum and the love child sat and cuddled on the beach. Mum got all misty-eyed and started talking about it being 'one of life's moments'. That's right Mum, it's the moment I took you all to the seaside at night.

Then Mum actually invited George to join us for a meal, although she insisted Blue and Skye sat between us. I'm not sure what she thought George and I were going to do; talk about judging people by your own standards!

227

George: Thank you, Mrs Foster, I'd love to come to dinner.

Mum: Actually, George, it's Ms Hammond.

Since when? I didn't know Mum had reverted to her maiden name. Ms? God! Now everyone will think she's a lesbian. Wait, does that make me Ellie Hammond? Actually, it's got quite a nice ring to it and makes me sound older. Anyway, even though he got her name wrong, I could tell that Mum was really impressed by George. She hates it when Poppy calls her Elaine.

Trevor: Great. I know, why don't we go to that little place that we took GM to? The owner was a bit rude but the food's great. Do you know it, George? It's just off the village square. It's got a tiny courtyard with just two tables. You go in through the bright red door. It was a real find; I'm surprised it's not in the *Rough Guide*.

George: Do you mean the place with the olive tree outside the gate?

Trevor: Yes, have you been there before?

George: Not really, no. That's where Mr and Mrs Hambouris live. It's not a restaurant, it's their home.

Even I laughed.

That night, we ended up at the pizzeria which I know was a little risky, but no one dropped any bombshells this time. I thought about announcing I was pregnant, just to get my own back but I didn't want to spoil my last night with George.

I didn't keep my side of the bargain with Poppy *(although I don't care about that now as she didn't keep her side either)* and George and I didn't even get close to 'doing it' *(in case the examiner is unsure and puts a call into the authorities as a*

228

precaution). I don't think we even reached second base, which is okay by me – I always was rubbish at rounders.

3.00pm

This is agony.

There's a dull, constant ache in my chest. Perhaps the strain of a long-distance relationship is giving me a heart attack. I'm missing George loads. He's promised to email me but it's not the same. Mum says he can come over for Christmas. Hopefully, he'll have put some weight on by then. Not sure what he'll think of Norbury. I might suggest he watches *I Am Legend* first, just to prepare him. Perhaps I can persuade the lovebirds to move somewhere cool, like Clapham.

Mum: Stop crying Ellie, it's unseemly.

No Mum, unseemly is your mother and her boyfriend discussing meeting in the toilets for a grope within earshot of her daughter. That's unseemly.

Mum: You know, I thought having a teenager was bad enough but having a teenager in love, now that's hell.

No Mum. Hell is your mother and her boyfriend announcing in the airport Departure Lounge that they are planning to have another love child. Call yourself a Geography teacher, Trevor! You clearly have no grasp of world population trends.

Me: But Mum, you're almost 40, you're too old (*we did the* *menopause briefly in Sex Ed: totally dull. Waste of time. I'll probably be dead by then).*

Mum: No, I'm not. Lots of women give birth later in life. And I've told you before, I'm 38!

Oh God, how repulsive! Madonna has a lot to answer for.

☆ ☆ ☆ ☆ ☆

4.00pm – Coming in to land at Heathrow airport.

The savages are tucking into some pistachio nuts. Love child has exchanged the Cheetos for Doritos. Mum is now halfway through *A Suitable Boy* but has had to pop a couple of Anadin as all that concentrating has given her a headache. Her arm is plastered with Nicotinell patches and she has promised that this time she is 'giving up the weed for good'. Trevor is looking very smug as he has managed to buy some contact lenses and a copy of *The Guardian* at the airport.

Trevor: Chile's environmental record is a disgrace.

Me: Right.

Trevor: The sooner we join the Euro the better, as far as I'm concerned.

Me: Right.

Trevor: Good grief.

Me: Right.

Trevor: I don't believe it! They've caught him.

Me: Who?

Trevor: The Norbury rapist.

Me: You're kidding.

Trevor: No, I'm not. It says here, police have arrested a man in connection with a series of attacks on women in Norbury, South London.

Fantastic! Freedom at last. Lucy Telling and I will be able to hang out at Abra-Kebab-Ra and flirt with Ali (*although as I already have a steady boyfriend, my relationship with him will of course remain strictly platonic*) without my mother trailing around after us, scowling at every male under the age of 85.

Me: Does that mean I'll be allowed to go out on my own?

Mum: Hold on a second, let's not jump to any conclusions. They might have the wrong man; no one's been charged yet. Miscarriages of justice take place all the time.

Trevor: Elaine, Ellie's nearly sixteen. She needs to stake her independence from time to time.

Mum: Well, I suppose so.

I catch Trevor's eye. He winks at me (*deliberately this time*) and gives me the thumbs up. How lame is that?! And for a minute there, I thought I liked him.

THE END

About the Author

Tina Orr Munro is a freelance journalist and writer. She lives in North Devon with her husband, four children and Wilfie, the dog.